DESERT DOORWAY

Max Daintry took a protective interest in
Jenny – young, ingenuous and visiting
Morocco for the first time. But Jenny
resented his atittude, and so, for different
reasons, did the lovely Frenchwoman who
employed her.

DESERT DOORWAY

by

PAMELA KENT

MILLS & BOON LIMITED
17–19 FOLEY STREET
LONDON W1A 1DR

First published *1956*
This edition *1974*

ISBN *0 263 71749 6*

Made and Printed in Great Britain by
Cox & Wyman Ltd, London, Reading
and Fakenham

CHAPTER ONE

THE big car nosed its way through the narrow streets, and on the back seat Jenny Armitage looked about her with widening eyes. After the glare of the open spaces, this network of narrow lanes into which they had plunged, with high walls shutting out the blinding light of the sun and the dazzle of white masonry, was an infinite relief. The only splashes of colour were provided by low doorways, set at intervals in the thick walls, and occasional cascades of blossom which overhung the walls and tapped gently upon the roof of the car as it slid silently below them.

All at once the car stopped outside a brightly-painted blue door set in an arched aperture. The chauffeur, who wore a pearl-grey livery to match the vehicle he drove, descended and addressed someone through an ornamental grille, and following the noise of bolts and bars, and the screech of what was evidently a very large key turning in a lock, the door swung inwards, and the chauffeur held open the rear door of the car for Jenny to alight.

She did so, feeling stiff and tired and most unsuitably clad in her tweed travelling suit. It was very light weight tweed, and for an English April it had been exactly right; but as she had worn it for a good many hours now, and flown many hundreds of miles through changing temperatures while still wearing it, it had also acquired a few creases, the consciousness of which in no way gave her the feeling of confidence she needed. In fact, as she followed the chauffeur who bore her very ordinary-looking suitcases under the arch, she looked a little scared and bewildered and apprehensive of what might lie ahead.

But almost immediately surprise banished a good deal of the apprehension, for who would have believed that on the far side of such a grim wall such a world of enchantment existed?

There was a brief passage which they traversed with echoing steps, and then they came out into a formal garden with marble columns and mosaic paths, hemmed in by a sea of white lilies and flaming hibiscus. There was the golden gleam of oranges, like balls of fire in the sunshine that fell brazenly from a cobalt-blue heaven, and a fountain shot diamond-spray high in the air and made a musical splashing noise as the falling water was caught again in a marble basin. It was a garden straight out of the *Arabian Nights*, and Jenny would have loved – in fact, she felt almost compelled – to pause for a few moments to admire it; but she was given no opportunity to do so, for an elderly, grave Berber servant emerged from an enclosed courtyard facing her, her luggage was handed over, and within a matter of seconds after that she was ushered into a marble-floored entrance hall, and from thence into a deliciously cool room furnished in European style as a library or study.

There were some beautiful leather chairs of deep chrome yellow, and the rugs on the polished floor had a jewel-like brilliance. Sandalwood tables were loaded with silver cigarette-boxes and bowls of scarlet flowers, there was a huge desk in one corner, and the walls were lined with books. On the desk a photograph stood in a very prominent position; a photograph in a kind of beaten silver frame of a woman with the flawless type of beauty possessed by Helen of Troy.

The Berber servant spoke beautiful, precise English, and he informed Jenny that Madame la Comtesse was out, but added that he had been instructed to ask her to rest, and to say that refreshments would be brought to her.

The refreshments took the form of mint tea and some very rich pastries coated thickly with almonds and chocolate; but although she found the mint tea refreshing, Jenny had no appetite at all for the pastries, and all she really longed to do once she was left alone was to sink gratefully into one of the deep leather chairs and feel the peace of the room flow round her. It was such a beautifully cool room that, once she had removed her jacket and the little hat which had been pressing on the red-gold waves of her hair like a constricting bandage for what seemed half a lifetime, she let out a sigh of pure relief, and felt much more like the Jenny Armitage who had left England, full of high hopes and excitement, less than twelve hours before.

And it was almost impossible now to believe that only a few days ago she had had no knowledge of what awaited her – no knowledge that life was suddenly about to open up before her like the petals of an exotic flower!

Not until the woman in the London agency had sent for her and said that she thought she would be exactly right for the post which had to be filled with as little delay as possible.

The requirements were uncomplicated. Someone who got on easily with young children, and could teach them English as well as a few other simple subjects, and maintain a certain amount of discipline as well. A well-brought-up woman belonging to a middle-class family, speaking good French, and preferably young, would be ideal. Jenny was nearly twenty-four, but because her eyes were the exact, deep shade of a periwinkle, and their expression was extraordinarily guileless, her small heart-shaped face looked usually rather eager, and she was slim and slightly built into the bargain, most people believed her to be much younger.

And, fortunately, she was quite free to go anywhere at almost a moment's notice – even to Morocco. Although when she heard that the services of an English governess were required by a French family in such a faraway-sounding place as Marrakesh, she was not at all certain that she had heard aright – not until she received confirmation that there was nothing wrong with her hearing powers. And then for the first time since the death of her adored father six months before she was able to feel glad that her acceptance of this unlooked-for job would cast no faintest shadow on anyone she might leave behind – for there was no one near and dear to her to be left behind! She was alone, quite alone in the world, and although for a young woman that might not be an entirely enviable position to be in, just now when the prospect of something new and untried was opening out before her the knowledge that she was without ties had its advantages.

At any rate, because of the ease with which she could cut adrift from all old landmarks, she was to be provided with a salary higher than anything she had ever earned before, and the expenses of her journey to Morocco had all been borne by her employer, whom she had yet to meet. And she had yet to meet her two pupils, also.

But although at the end of her journey, largely as the result of travel-weariness, she was not quite so confident about meeting them, after she had sat for a while in an atmosphere so soothing to jaded nerves most of her fears became lulled, and the whole thing once more appeared to her rather like an exciting adventure, whatever way it might turn out. It was quite possible she might not suit – she might even be too young for the post, or the children might be difficult, or they might not take to her, or she to them! This house was very luxurious, but it remained to be seen what tasks she would have to perform in it, and they might not be the kind of task she would have chosen for herself.

But she was prepared to believe that she *could* perform them.

On the wall directly facing her there hung an exquisitely delicate landscape painted in watercolours – a tiny bit of southern France, with some terraced vineyards and a glimpse of a house with pepper-box towers. Behind her french windows stood open to a kind of enclosed patio, where another fountain played, and the sound of the continuously falling water was so soothing that, after listening to it consciously for several minutes, she began to feel slightly drowsy, and actually

9

closed her eyes for about half a minute.

At least, she would have been prepared to swear that it was only for half a minute, for when she opened her eyes again as if something had jerked them open by means of unseen wires she knew exactly where she was, and she knew also why she was there and whom she was waiting to see.

But someone had startled her from behind, and a careless masculine voice was the cause of her awakening. The voice was deep and pleasant and provocative, and it was also faintly caressing. A man's shadow was bending over her, and she felt a quick kiss on her bright hair. She knew it was a kiss, although it was light as a feather, because of the warm breath that so unexpectedly fanned her cheek, and she caught the faint, masculine aroma of shaving-cream and cigarette-smoke before the provocative voice exclaimed:

'So I'm fortunate for once and find you alone! Wake up, Célestine, my sweet! The time for siesta is over—!'

And then a horrified exclamation followed:

'Good heavens! Who – who are you?' he demanded bluntly. 'And why have you got red hair?'

CHAPTER TWO

THERE had been occasions in Jenny's life when the fact that there was a tinge of red in her hair had annoyed her, especially during her schooldays, when those who were not her bosom friends had been known to refer to her as "Carrots". But never until now had anyone actually demanded, and on a note of unmistakable resentment, *why* she had red hair. She was so angry — and so indignant because someone had attempted to kiss her while she slept (or appeared to sleep!) — that she sprang up with one swift movement like a young and very startled mountain goat.

'I *beg* your pardon!' she exclaimed.

Although she was prepared to deny that she had indulged in anything more than the briefest of naps, she felt a sensation of confusion and uncertainty, which threatened to overwhelm her as she stared at the man confronting her. He was so tall that she felt herself dwarfed by him, and rather elegantly spare. He wore a suit of fine white drill— and his hair was almost startlingly black by contrast, and in the dimness of the room his eyes appeared black too. Although he had a slightly swarthy skin which made him look distinctly foreign, his accent was unmistakably English, and the arrogant line of his mouth and the square lift to his jaw also proclaimed a certain insularity which belongs, by universal consent, to dwellers in the British Isles.

'Granted,' he replied swiftly, the surprise vanishing

11

from his eyes, and a lazy look of amusement taking its place, while a slow smile parted his lips over very white teeth. 'But do sit down again,' he begged. 'It isn't good to jump up like that when you've been wrapped in the arms of Morpheus. And as for begging my pardon – why, surely, the boot's on the other foot?'

'It – it certainly ought to be!' Jenny answered, with a quiver in her voice. 'And what has the colour of my hair got to do with you? And in any case, it isn't red!'

'Isn't it?' His eyes dwelt on it – those dark, cynically amused eyes which she was later to discover were a very curious and intense grey, rather like the cool pebbles on a remote northern shore – and a gleam of appreciation lit them. 'Well, perhaps you're right. It could be a kind of burnished gold, or some people might describe it as chestnut. I've seen ripe, glossy chestnuts that had much in common with the tint of your hair. On the other hand, the painter Titian might have been interested in it—'

'Does it matter?' she demanded swiftly, a frown creasing her forehead because she was so much affronted by his cool impertinence, and so unprepared to deal with it. 'Just now you – you—'

'Saluted you in a manner hardly in keeping with so brief an acquaintance?'

'You obviously made a mistake,' she said coldly, 'but even so, an apology would hardly be out of place.'

'I couldn't agree more,' he assured her calmly, and produced a thin gold cigarette-case from his pocket and offered it to her with a ceremonious bow as she sank back unwillingly into her chair. She shook her head in an aloof manner. 'No? Then I hope you won't object if I do, because you took me so much by surprise just now that I haven't quite got over it. I was quite certain you were Célestine—'

'Célestine?'

'Madame la Comtesse de St. Alais.' His smile baffled her, not only because it was slightly one-sided, but because there was a kind of satirical enjoyment in it. 'You and she both run to the same controversial shade of hair—'

'Oh,' she exclaimed, as if enlightened, 'then you must be – you must be the Comte de St. Alais?'

'I'm afraid that by no means automatically follows,' he told her, seating himself on the arm of a chair and regarding her with such a mocking curve to his lips, and such a cool look of mockery in his eyes that she felt her face suddenly start to flame. 'However, Célestine and I are quite good friends, and we occasionally greet one another in a fashion frequently reserved for good friends, and that I happened to drop a kiss on the top of your head was merely, if you'll take the broad view, a little unfortunate. And, in any case, I do apologize, and if there is anything I can do apart from that to convince you that it is quite unlikely ever to happen again—?'

She felt that he was laughing at her in a most annoying fashion, and her colour spread wildly.

'Have you any idea when the Comtesse is likely to return?' she asked, through stiff and disapproving lips.

'I'm afraid I haven't. I had no idea she was out, or I wouldn't have wended my way here this afternoon. However, I shouldn't think she'd be long.' And then all at once enlightenment seemed to descend upon him. 'I know!' he exclaimed. 'You must be the new governess?'

'I am,' she admitted.

'Straight out from England?'

'Yes.'

He placed his cigarette between his lips and drew thoughtfully upon it for several seconds while he studied her quite openly with something distinctly interested in his eyes.

'First trip abroad?' he asked.

'Yes,' she admitted again, and slipped hastily into the jacket of her suit before he could offer any assistance, and fastened it primly, while she kept her eyes deliberately lowered in order to avoid meeting his gaze.

'I'm not a seer,' he told her, 'and neither have I any unusual powers, but I'd place your background as that of a country vicarage, and further hazard the guess that you haven't been away from it for very long? You've been accustomed to helping your father with his sermons – typing them with two fingers on an antiquated typewriter! – and helping your mother with the flowers and the Overseas Missions? You were very much liked by the people in the village, and you're frightfully good at organizing Jumble Sales, and the main prop of the Amateur Dramatic Society. You're not too bad, either, at getting up concerts when it's necessary to raise the wind for a new church organ!'

Her long eyelashes, which were very dark save where they appeared to be dusted with gold-dust at the tips, flew up, and she stared at him with eyes that were so deeply blue they were almost violet.

'H-how did you know?' she demanded.

He laughed at her openly.

'I didn't know — but just by looking at you I felt certain I couldn't be making a mistake!' And then, even more mockingly: 'Tell me, did you suddenly feel the urge to escape from it all? — to stretch your wings? Is that what you're doing now?'

'My father died,' she said, and for a moment her fingers shook as she clasped them together tightly in her lap, and to her own extreme annoyance her voice was not altogether steady, either. 'And my mother died about eighteen months ago.'

'I — see,' he said, and then he stood up abruptly and wandered over to the open window for a few moments and stood looking out at the spraying fountain. When he returned to her his voice had lost the mocking note. 'Did you fly out?'

'Yes.'

'Feeling tired?'

'Not particularly.' But she suddenly knew that she was tired — tired and a little deflated. And she longed for someone to show her to a room where she could get out of her hot tweed suit and into something cool, and perhaps have a bath, and bathe her eyes with a cooling lotion because they were still suffering from the assault made upon them by staring white buildings and brazen blue skies after the half-tones and the cool grey skies of England. Also, she wanted to be left alone again — completely alone until she felt more like herself.

'My name's Max Daintry,' the man told her, in an ordinary conversational tone, 'and you'll probably see quite a lot of me if you stay out here. I've formed a kind of habit of haunting this house.' He paused. 'If you'd like me to ring for the servant and tell him to show you to your room—'

'Oh, no—' she was beginning, feeling this would be taking rather a lot on himself, when they both caught the sound of footsteps crossing the flagged floor of the hall at the same time, and as they looked round expectantly the door that was also set in an arched aperture was flung open, and a tall and very beautiful woman stood looking critically in at them.

Jenny realized at once that this was the Comtesse de St. Alais – the 'Célestine' whose hair was very similar to her own – and she stood up automatically to greet her, to acknowledge herself in the presence of one who had undertaken to pay her quite a large salary.

Max Daintry, with a return of his casual, mocking manner, strolled towards her, and the Comtesse's eyes, after resting for a brief moment on Jenny, seemed to become glued to his face. There was something avid and almost fierce about the way those huge brown eyes – golden-brown, rather like amber, with tiny, greenish lights in them – under spectacular eyelashes, hung as if compelled upon the cool, grey glance of the Englishman. She said softly, in English, but with a very noticeable accent:

'Max, you annoying man! Why did you not let me know you would be here this afternoon?'

'Because I wasn't certain I would be here.' He returned her look with a strangely inscrutable little smile and a brief, flickering glance at her superbly graceful figure, clothed in something cool and green like lime-blossom, while the contrast afforded by shoes, gloves and an enormous cartwheel hat, all in speckless white, was most effective. And under the cartwheel hat the bronze-gold hair – several tones more brilliant than Jenny's, because it received the constant attention of experts – formed soft little tendrils that lay like golden feathers on her white brow and the smooth perfection of her cheek.

'If only you had telephoned!'

'There was nothing very much to telephone about.'

Jenny, feeling acutely uncomfortable, was quite sure her eyes reproached him.

Then, as if all at once it struck her that Jenny would no longer be completely ignored, the Comtesse walked across the room to her. She said, in a tone of almost icy reserve and aloofness:

'Miss Armitage?'

Jenny admitted her identity at once, and felt her heart sink at the same time.

'I'm sorry I was not here when you arrived, Miss Armitage, but I trust you have been properly looked after?' Her eyes dropped to the untasted pastries on the tray. 'Perhaps you have not been here very long?'

'I don't know, I – not very long—' Jenny was a little confused, because she felt there was an implication in that suggestion, and she had no real idea how long it was since she had arrived. But Max Daintry came up behind her employer and contributed the information that they had been getting to know one another, but he had had no idea a governess was expected today. And as yet he had not been formally introduced to Miss Armitage, who, after all, was a fellow countrywoman of his.

Célestine looked at him with strange, brooding eyes.

'And yet you have admitted that you have been getting to know one another,' she said. 'Is it necessary after that to be formally introduced?'

'I think so,' Max murmured back, and the Comtesse responded in her clipped, attractive, and slightly husky English:

'Miss Armitage, this is Mr. Daintry, a near neighbour of ours. Max, this is Miss Jenny Armitage. But as she has come out here from England to look after the children, and for no other purpose, it is scarcely likely that you will see a great deal of one another,' with the coolest of smiles curving the lovely lips.

'Dear me!' the Englishman exclaimed with a wry look. 'I hope that doesn't mean you are going to shut Miss Armitage up in the nursery suite and starve her of all other companionship? If you do that you'll have her running back to her country vicarage.'

The Comtesse looked at Jenny as if she was trying to decide whether she really had all the simplicity a clergyman's daughter should have, or whether the *ingénue* look was a mere façade. And then Daintry's smooth voice cut in more decisively:

'And I think it would be a good plan if you allowed Miss Armitage to be shown to her room. She has admitted to me that she's a bit tired, and one never feels too bright after a journey.'

'Of course.'

The Comtesse touched a bell on a small table near to her, and then more or less turned her back on Jenny. 'You will dine with us tonight, Max?' she asked eagerly.

'I don't know whether I ought to—'

Jenny turned away and stared first at the view of southern France on the wall, and then at the photograph of the beautiful woman on the desk. It was easy enough now to recognize in the photograph the perfect features of her new employer, and if anything it barely did Célestine justice. Only a coloured mezzotint could do absolute justice to her ivory and gold loveliness, and even that would have none of the living, breathing perfection of the original – or so Jenny decided, as she tried to shut her ears to the conversation of the other two, which certainly concerned her not at all.

The Berber servant appeared, and his mistress directed him to take Jenny to her room, and to see that she had everything she wanted. And she added condescendingly to the girl herself:

'Perhaps when you have had an opportunity to rest and change you will like to meet the children? They are eagerly looking forward to meeting you, but a visit to their grandmother this afternoon has put them into a state of rather wild excitement. You may find them a little unruly. But they are not normally difficult to manage.'

'I'm quite sure they're not,' Jenny managed awkwardly, and then caught the eyes of Max Daintry upon her again, with that amused, half-derisive look in them that was so oddly confusing. She answered his '*Au revoir*, Miss Armitage – don't let those little horrors make rings round you!' with an unintelligible murmur, and then made her escape as quickly as she could, following in the wake of the servant.

CHAPTER THREE

THE house, she was to discover later, was huge, with corridors branching off in all directions, and much evidence of a great deal of tastefully expended wealth. It was furnished with a mixture of Moorish art and European luxury, and many of the pictures and the carpets, the wall tapestries and the examples of period furniture collected from a good many corners of the globe, were, she realized, probably almost priceless.

But on this first night of her arrival, after she had left the library behind her, she was suddenly so conscious of a dispiriting tiredness that the impressions she gained were vague in the extreme. Not only did weariness seem all at once to drag at her limbs, but a curious mental flatness had taken the place of her earlier high hopes and optimism. She attributed the latter in part to the acute dislike she had taken to Max Daintry – a man who dropped kisses on to the head of a married woman (or that was what he had imagined he was doing when he had taken her, Jenny, by surprise!) and had mocking, disparaging eyes, was hardly the type to inspire confidence in a newly-arrived governess – and also the Comtesse de St. Alais herself was something in the nature of a rather pronounced disappointment.

She was too beautiful and too hostile – barely concealing contempt for a girl who had to earn her own living behind the thinnest veneer of very distant politeness. Unless it was that, coming upon Jenny apparently cosily closeted with a man whom she herself regarded as a very particular friend, she had been vexed and put out.

In which case, what were the sentiments of the Comte de St. Alais, and how soon would he make his appearance on Jenny's immediate horizon? Which reminded her that very soon now she would be making the acquaintance of her two future charges.

Her rooms, when they reached them – and she was surprised to discover that she had been allocated something in the nature of a suite – were so pleasant that for a few minutes, as she looked about her, she was conscious of nothing but a sudden uprising of pleasure. There was a very large bedroom with a balcony overlooking one of the central courtyards, with cool colonnades supported by marble pillars, and a rectangular pool on which water-lilies floated; and separated from it by an archway hung with striped Moorish curtains and a divan piled high with cushions. Jenny's appreciative eyes lighted upon a beautiful little Empire writing-table at which she could write her letters, and here again the outlook was over the courtyard. French windows admitted to both balconies, and there were long wicker lounging chairs, and striped sun-blinds to be drawn against the heat of the day.

She was also delighted to discover that she had her own bathroom, with a deep and wonderfully luxurious bath, and unlimited quantities of boiling water when she turned on the chromium taps.

She was quick to take advantage of the bathroom, and was slipping into one of the coolest dresses her somewhat limited wardrobe contained – a flowered cotton with a background of lavender-blue, and a wide white collar – when without even a knock the door opened, and the Comtesse came into the room.

She had made no alteration to her own appearance as yet, but she cast an openly critical glance at Jenny, and surprised the latter by expressing approval of what she was wearing.

'You'll find the nights here are very cold,' she said, 'so if you do have occasion to go out after dinner remember that it's advisable to wear a wrap. And I shall expect you always to dine with us – unless, of course,' with a smile, 'someone invites you out to dinner – and my husband likes to see the children at luncheon, so I shall expect you and them to lunch with us. And now I suggest that you come along with me to the children's quarters.'

Jenny followed at once, and as the wing which housed the children was not very far from her own she was soon gravely shaking hands with a couple of precocious infants who were sitting up side by side in exactly similar beds in a large, airy room beautifully decorated in pastel tints.

Simone, who was four, had a mass of jet ringlets, and enormous dark eyes that were capable of staring with deceptive solemnity for astonishingly long periods; but Louis, the boy – two years his sister's senior – had his mother's fair colouring, and looked like an angel with his longish hair that twisted into soft curls, and eyes of clear, pale honey-gold. Both children wore expensive nightwear of heavy silk, and their bed sheets and pillow-cases were of crêpe-de-chine. A Moorish girl who was introduced to Jenny as Nerida was keeping them entertained with picture books until the moment arrived when they were expected to lie down and go to sleep, and after a brief, interested exchange of glances Jenny decided that she and this sixteen-year-old girl would probably get on very well, since, although she looked delicate and pretty as a shy mountain doe, she also looked intelligent, and spoke excellent Mission-school English.

Célestine allowed the children to make a considerable fuss of her before she finally said good night to them, but when they started to get a little out of hand she spoke to them sharply. They chorused, 'Yes, Mamma,' when she told them to lie down and shut their eyes, but Louis kept his open long enough to observe that Jenny was watching him with amusement, and he grinned at her engagingly. 'Mademoiselle Armitage stay with us,' he said in French, as if he half hoped the demand would be acceded to. But the Comtesse replied crisply:

'Certainly not. Mademoiselle Armitage is coming downstairs to dinner, and in any case you are to speak English with her and not French. You understand?'

'*Oui*, Maman,' came the reply – and then was quickly changed to 'Yes, Mamma.'

As they went out of the nursery door the Comtesse explained to the new governess:

'I wish the children to speak English perfectly as quickly as possible. Their grandmother – my husband's mother – is English, and that is one reason why I want them to become thoroughly accustomed to her language. I would like you to concentrate on improving their idiom.'

'Of course, if that is what you wish,' Jenny replied, and then was allowed to return to her own apartments until a musical-toned gong throbbed through the house and warned her that it was time to go downstairs.

She had been secretly filled with a kind of dread of meeting Max Daintry again that night, but he had evidently decided against accepting the Comtesse's invitation, for he was not in the dining-room when she entered it. But the Comte de St. Alais was standing at the head of a long table loaded with silver and cut-glass and flowers, and as soon as Jenny entered the room he moved towards her and held out a welcoming hand.

'How do you do, Miss Armitage?' he said, and his English was without any trace of an accent – which was not, perhaps, so surprising, if his mother was English.

He was a slenderly built man of middle height, and although his hair was very dark there were a few betraying touches of white at the temples. He had dark, gentle, kindly eyes – in fact, they were beautiful eyes, a little like his small daughter's, but much more capable of revealing every passing emotion, and very thickly lashed. Jenny thought he was quite strikingly handsome, and she also thought he looked particularly well in a white dinner-jacket, and the manner in which he waved her to the table and saw that she was comfortably seated was distinctly the manner of a *grand seigneur*.

And once she was seated, although his wife was seated facing him at the bottom of the table, and was looking like a remote golden goddess in a gown of gold

24

brocade that caught every brilliant ray of the light from the swinging chandelier above their heads, he directed all his conversation at Jenny, and asked her considerately about her journey, and how much of the world she had already seen. When she confessed that this was her first trip abroad he smiled – a smile that warmed her heart a little – and then observed that since she was obviously very young she had plenty of time ahead of her to see more of the globe if she wished.

Célestine, whose face was so void of expression that it might have been carved out of alabaster, flickered her eyelashes for a moment as she looked across at Jenny.

'Miss Armitage is twenty-four,' she remarked coolly deliberately, 'and at twenty-four I had already been married for six years! But in France we mature more quickly than you do in England. Even so, at twenty-four you should be thoroughly capable of looking after yourself, Miss Armitage.'

'I – I hope so,' Jenny found herself stammering, in faint confusion.

The Comte's eyes continued to dwell on her.

'Perhaps they made a mistake on your birth certificate when you were born,' he suggested, smiling again. 'You do not look to me as if you are yet out of your teens.'

'There is nothing more deceptive than looks,' his wife interposed, with an edge to her voice like a sliver of ice. 'The important thing is that Miss Armitage is capable of doing all the things we expect her to do now that she has arrived, and amongst those things I hope you are capable of maintaining discipline, Miss Armitage? Louis must be taught to recognize authority before he is sent away to school, and as he is nearly six that will not be long now. Another six months – or a year at the outside.'

'But he is only a baby!' Jenny found herself exclaiming, in a shocked voice.

'Babies quickly develop into men,' Célestine remarked, and stared – once more without any expression on her face – at the portion of breast of chicken cooked in a wine sauce that had been placed in front of her by a white-robed servant.

Stealing a quick glance at the Comte, Jenny thought that the line of his lips tightened, but she could not be sure of this. She only knew that after that, although he continued to talk to her smoothly, there was no longer very much expression in his eyes, and they looked darker, and much deeper, than they had done before.

After dinner Célestine was carried away in a large and glittering car to some evening function which she was attending without her husband, and the Comte withdrew to his library, after making sure that Jenny really preferred to be granted permission to retire upstairs to her own rooms.

Jenny, as a matter of fact, was glad to regain the freedom and the isolation of her own apartments, for the long-drawn-out dinner in the superbly appointed dining-room, with its French tapestries, and its all too revealing crystal chandeliers, had, on top of her exhausting day, sapped the few remnants of her strength and energy.

She had felt, while the dinner progressed, that she had acted as a kind of buffer between two people who were constantly – if not, perhaps, openly – at war, and the feeling had been a bigger strain than anything she had ever experienced before.

In her sitting-room she threw open the french window and stepped out on to the balcony. It was bitterly cold – so cold that she gasped for a moment, and then quickly withdrew in search of a wrap – and when she returned to the balcony rail she was huddled in a warm overcoat.

She looked upwards at the sky – so brilliantly blue, even though the light had long since faded, that she knew she had never seen anything quite like it before. It had a strange quality of depth and luminosity, and the stars that hung in it like lamps looked as if they could be snatched out of it if the invisible threads by which they were suspended in space could be severed. Then she looked downwards at the rectangular pool on which the water-lilies floated, and she saw the stars reflected there, too, like lamps that were maintaining their brilliance under water.

A keen wind blew against her face and stirred her hair, and although it had the coolness of melting snows it was perfumed by the breath of the golden oranges that were growing all around her under the curtain of the night. There was something vaguely exciting about the perfume, and she drew it in in deep breaths.

Then, just before she decided that if she was not to catch a chill on her first night in Morocco she had better return to her sitting-room, she thought she saw someone moving in the white marble colonnade facing her. It was a black and white figure, slenderly graceful, and as it moved she saw the glowing tip of a cigarette. She decided that the only person it could be was the Comte, and that he was probably watching her on her balcony and disapproving of her heedless risking of a chill, so she promptly withdrew into the flood of soft amber light behind her, and then stopped to secure the window.

But as she went into her bedroom and started to undress – wondering what it would be like to sleep in the ornate French bed – she thought of Célestine, the lovely Comtesse de St. Alais, and she found herself wondering about her and – Max Daintry.

Had Célestine really gone to spend the evening with friends of both herself and her husband? Or had she gone to meet Max Daintry? Were they perhaps both spending the evening at the house of a mutual friend?

Jenny felt suddenly acutely sorry for the Comte de St. Alais.

CHAPTER FOUR

IT was exactly a week after her arrival in Marrakesh that Jenny saw Max Daintry again. She was enjoying her first free morning – that is to say, having handed the children over to the care of Nerida, she had been given permission to enjoy an hour or so of sight-seeing and shopping – and having been dropped by the Comtesse in the Place du 7 Septembre she had found her way gradually to the Djemaâ el Fna, the huge market-place. She was standing as if awed by the sights on all sides of her when she heard a voice she immediately recognized utter her name from behind. And it was odd, because the first time she had ever heard that voice its owner had had the advantage of coming upon her from behind.

'Miss Jenny Armitage!' the voice exclaimed. And then more disapprovingly: 'But why are you here alone?'

Jenny looked up at him a trifle vaguely. The Comtesse, who was on her way to a jeweller to recover a set of bracelets that had been entrusted to him for cleaning, had promised to send the car back for her at one o'clock. But unaccustomed to the ways of Moorish life though she was, it had struck the younger girl as a little strange that she should be light-heartedly abandoned to her own devices in entirely unfamiliar surroundings for so lengthy a period as a couple of hours, without receiving anything in the nature of advice beforehand.

29

'I – why, I – this is my off-duty –'

'Off-duty?' he echoed. Still looking up at him she could see that he was frowning, but in the brilliant sunshine it was impossible to make any mistake about the colour of his eyes. They were most decidedly grey – a hard, clear grey in which the shadows of his wiry black eyelashes were reflected. 'And are you usually turned loose during your off-duty periods?'

'This is the first off-duty period I've had.'

'I see,' he said, and taking her by the elbow removed her from the path of a blind beggar who was tapping loudly with his stick to warn of his approach, and staring upwards at the brazen blue of the sky with empty sockets of eyes.

'Oh!' Jenny exclaimed, and felt herself shuddering inwardly.

Max Daintry looked down at her with an odd smile curving his lips.

'You'll see pleasant sights and unpleasant sights if you remain out here,' he told her, and then directed her attention to the white ranges of the High Atlas beyond the city walls, incredibly beautiful with the sunlight pouring over them, and the blue sky behind them. The walls of the city were red – a soft rose-red, like coral – and nearer at hand were thousands of tall palms, soaring upwards in the clear air. Jenny felt her temporary repulsion fade, and then once again she looked about her at the – from her point of view – extraordinary sights that had been fascinating her before.

There were white-robed figures squatting on the ground around snake-charmers and story-tellers, musicians and actors performing comic plays. There were 'holy men', repulsively dirty, contorting their bodies, and stamping frenziedly to the rhythm of small, oblong, hand-beaten drums which filled the square with an incessant throbbing; and medicine-men surrounded by their grotesque medicines: the skins of lizards, claws of leopards, skulls of foxes, and any number of bottles of evil-looking liquids. And in addition to this strange, motley collection there were various sellers of goods — old-clothes sellers, water-sellers, sellers of sickly sweets.

Round the sides of the square there were open-fronted shops, stocked with quantities of things likely to appeal to Europeans, such as fake jewellery, cheap perfume, plastic combs, belts, and even mackintoshes. There were open-sided tents where fish was roasted over a brazier, and trestle tables at which customers sat devouring roast chestnuts and corncobs, and the smell of the various frying foods mingled with the heady smell of jasmine and those wax-white lilies which Jenny had already seen growing in profusion.

She was so fascinated that she could have remained gazing at these amazing sights indefinitely, but once again Daintry took her by the arm and led her, without asking her permission, towards a parked car near the centre of the square.

'If you want to see the sights I can show them to you,' he said. 'But first of all what about having some coffee somewhere?'

'Coffee?' Once again she gazed at him vaguely, for that wild cacophony of noises, made up of the many raucous voices raised against one another, and the incessant throbbing of the drums, was making a violent assault on her unaccustomed ears.

'Yes. And I'd like to talk to you, if you don't mind.'

She looked up at him rather more sharply as he handed her into the car – like all the cars she had so far seen in Marrakesh, luxurious and expensive.

'Is there anything particular you wish to talk to me about?' she asked, by no means certain that she wished to spend any time at all in his company.

'There is – one thing,' he admitted, piloting the car through the maze of streets which formed the *medina*, or native quarter. And then, with a much more casual air: 'How do you like it here in Marrakesh?'

'It's early days yet to form an opinion, isn't it?' she counter-questioned.

He glanced at her with the mocking smile she remembered.

'Which means that the little girl from the country vicarage is by no means certain that she does like it – isn't that it? Or perhaps she's just a bit afraid of life in the raw! Although life in the St. Alais household should be comfortable enough.'

'It is,' she admitted stiffly.

'We must take you for a trip up into the High Atlas one of these days,' he said, 'and then you'll forget about the Moroccan slums. And Marrakesh is a kind of doorway to the desert – not the real desert, for that isn't to be come upon this side of the Atlas – but parched and arid enough to be exciting if that sort of thing appeals to you?' She felt that he silently added the words 'Valentino stuff!' as he sent her another mocking

32

glance, as if she was a raw teenager, secretly expecting adventure.

She felt herself colouring, and decided that there was little about him she could like, and something of which she could actively disapprove.

They drew up outside a very large hotel set in beautiful gardens encircled by high walls. Jenny did not know that this was the leading luxury hotel in Marrakesh, the Mamounia, which means 'garden of monkeys', but as she had been expecting to be taken for coffee to somewhere more suggestive of a café – perhaps a Moorish type of café – she was a little surprised.

As Daintry handed her out of the car he looked at her closely. She was wearing a candy-pink linen dress, and above it the deep blue of her eyes, and the peculiarly flawless texture of her skin, seemed somehow enhanced by the suggestion of an English hedge-rose. She had a very youthful, soft curve to her chin, and her mouth was both flower-like and ardent. And against the white of her hat her hair was very definitely chestnut.

'I think you'll fit in better here than in one of the cafés,' he said.

She did not answer, but followed him into the hotel, her eyes opening wide at the enormous lounges and public rooms. They reminded her of a super Hollywood film-set, but the atmosphere was cool and restful, and after the noise and confusion of the Djemaâ el Fna she was glad of an opportunity to forget it for a short while.

Their coffee was brought, and once again she ob-

33

served that he was studying her almost earnestly. He offered her a cigarette, and although she refused at first she changed her mind and accepted hurriedly when she saw the faint, amused smile slide into his eyes, and knew what he was thinking.

The vicar's daughter was not used to smoking, and that meant she was still very inexperienced! She saw his white teeth revealed in an open smile as he held a light to the tip of her cigarette, and knew that he had even read her thoughts – and recognized her reaction!

He was not the type of man she should be spending any time with at all!

He lay back in his chair, and she noticed how extremely impeccable was his thin white suit, and how admirably tailored. By contrast with the whiteness his skin looked very brown, and his hair had the sleek blackness of a raven's wing. But for his English voice and name and those not particularly English grey eyes he might easily have been French, or even Italian.

'If I make a suggestion,' he said suddenly, surprising her, 'are you likely to be very much annoyed with me?'

She had dropped her eyes to her coffee, but she looked up quickly and met the cool blankness of his deliberate stare.

'Surely that,' she replied uncertainly, 'depends upon the nature of the suggestion you are going to make?'

'Nothing in the least personal,' he assured her, a cold smile flickering round his definitely handsome mouth. 'Only something in connection with your own well-being – future well-being, perhaps I should say!'

'Well?' she asked, her eyes widening considerably.

'And although I'm gong to give you a piece of advice, there is absolutely no reason why you should take it.'

'Did you bring me here because you wanted to give me advice?' she asked more curiously, as he seemed in no hurry to lay his advice before her.

'Partly – although, of course, you are a country-woman of mine, aren't you?' with a mocking smile. 'And we don't get many of your type out here – certainly not in positions of subordination, shall we say, in the houses of the local great?'

'By which you mean the Comte and Comtesse de St. Alais?'

'I mean the Comte and Comtesse de St. Alais – and my advice to you, the suggestion I wish to make to you, is that you cease to look upon them as employers, and go home to England! You can hand in your notice at any time, I take it? You don't have to serve a full month, or anything of that sort? How long have you been here now? A week?'

'A week today,' she answered him stiffly, and then added with hardly repressed indignation and amazement: 'I never heard such an impertinent suggestion in my life! And not only because it concerns anything so vital to me as my job, but because you profess to be a friend of the St. Alais's, and yet you would deprive them of their governess!'

Her voice trembled with indignation.

'I was afraid you would take it like that,' he said, and signed to the waiter to bring more coffee.

But Jenny had no desire for any more coffee, and she

pushed away the half-empty cup that was already in front of her.

'I'll have to go now,' she said, preparing to rise. 'The Comtesse is sending the car for me.'

'You've plenty of time,' he told her almost lazily, glancing at his watch, 'and, if I know anything about Célestine, the car will be late!' And then, with sudden, abrupt seriousness – icily cool seriousness, because his face as well was hard and expressionless – 'Wouldn't you like to hear at least one reason why I think it advisable that you should go home to England?'

'No, I don't think so.' But she was staring at him in amazement. How could he make such a suggestion and expect her to pay any attention to it? 'For one thing, I can't afford to give up my job, and for another, I am on a month to month arrangement—'

'That can easily be put right,' he told her in the same distant manner. 'But can you honestly tell me that the job has come up to all your expectations?'

'Yes' – a little defiantly – 'it has – in a way! I love the children, and already we are great friends . . .'

'And do you find yourself just as much drawn to Célestine?' he inquired with very noticeable dryness.

'She is quite a considerate employer; she doesn't interfere,' Jenny replied truthfully.

'And the Comte? How do you like the Comte?'

'He is *very* considerate.'

'Ah, yes,' the Englishman murmured, as if he found this piece of information interesting, 'I've no doubt he would be – and will probably continue to be!'

Her eyes, with their attractive suggestion of violets hidden in the depths of a shadowy wood, stared at him resentfully.

'And are you trying to tell me that the Comtesse will cease to be after a time?'

He shook his head.

'I am trying to tell you nothing. I am merely asking you – suggesting to you – to go home! More than that I cannot say, in your own best interests you should regard this Moroccan adventure as nothing more than an adventure which has misfired, turn your back on it and forget all about it as quickly as you can. Believe me, I wouldn't give you this advice if I wasn't sure you are the wrong type altogether to have hit upon this governessing post, which is not your cup of tea at all.'

'You mean that I am not capable of giving the maximum amount of efficiency in return for my salary?' she asked with dangerous softness.

'Not at all. I am quite sure you are extremely efficient, and the St. Alais infants have probably taken to you – but that is all beside the point.'

'What is the point, then?' she insisted.

'I have told you – it's not the job for you. You are too young—'

'I am twenty-four. The Comtesse particularly asked for someone young, and so far she has found nothing about me to complain of.'

He was regarding her beneath very black and frowning brows, and she felt sure she had driven him into a corner.

'If your father was alive I am sure he would not have approved of your coming out here.'

'No, but he isn't,' she said, with a sigh in the words.

And then she added more stiffly: 'And that is a definite reflection on the integrity of the Comte.'

Daintry ignored this, and then asked almost impatiently:

'Will you be guided by me and go back to the kind of people you understand, and amongst whom you can find any number of jobs similar to the one you are holding down now?'

Jenny found herself frowning at him just as he was frowning at her, and all at once she felt as if a flood of daylight had poured over her.

Of course, she thought, the reason why he wanted her to go was because he personally did not wish her to remain where she was! She might in time become a nuisance – a hindrance to his 'friendship' with Célestine. Her sympathies began to go out towards the Comte. It must be obvious to the meanest intelligence that the latter and his wife were estranged, and – as Jenny unfortunately already knew – the mother of Simone and Louis was in the habit of permitting herself to be kissed by Max Daintry, and she had looked at him with eyes of hungry possessiveness which no one could possibly have misunderstood . . . !

The meaning of Daintry's desire to remove an observant English governess from the path was very clear!

'If you don't mind,' Jenny said, rising in quite a dignified manner, 'I really will go now. And,' looking at him with cool scorn in her eyes, 'however guilty your own conscience, Mr. Daintry, I can assure you that you need have no fear of me whatsoever. I shall not be tempted to act as a spy on behalf of the children's father, and whatever you and the Comtesse de St. Alais choose to do is no concern of mine.'

She moved towards the entrance, and realized that he was following hard at her heels. When she ventured to turn and look at him over her shoulder she saw that his face appeared to have lost a considerable amount of its tan, and that he was almost white with anger, while his eyes frightened her for a moment.

'Perhaps it will be as well if you forget our conversation of this morning,' he said, and suddenly forged ahead of her and led the way out to his car. He held the door open for her, and when she was seated beside him he started up the engine and drove her back to the Place du 7 Septembre, where they saw that the Comtesse's car, with the grey liveried chauffeur at the wheel, was drawn up awaiting her. Jenny's wrist-watch indicated that it was a quarter past one.

'Thank you for the coffee,' she said, as she climbed stiffly down from her seat beside the wheel of Daintry's car, 'and thank you,' she added, with a dryness which was marred by her shocked realization that she was a quarter of an hour late, 'for your advice!'

'Forget it,' he advised curtly, and he didn't wait until the chauffeur had started up the grey car before his own engine purred to life again and he shot across the square like an arrogant streak of controlled dark crimson fury picked out with a great deal of chromium and an English number plate.

And, as Jenny realized, he hadn't even said goodbye to her!

CHAPTER FIVE

WHEN she reached the St. Alais house she was so conscious of being late for lunch that she was almost in a panic. This was the first time she had been permitted the indulgence of a few hours off duty, and she had kept the Comtesse's chauffeur waiting, and worse than that the family would already be at lunch in the great dining-room, and her entrance in the middle of the meal would look extremely bad, even if one took a light view of it.

But she had to hasten up to her room to tidy herself and wash the stickiness of the morning from her hands and face before she could join the others, and by the time she had hastily re-made up her face another ten minutes had sped by. She descended the stairs with a quaking heart, and entered the dining-room ready to express sincerest apologies.

But the Comte — who, as usual, was seated at the head of the table — said to her very pleasantly, as he immediately stood up:

'Oh, hello, Miss Armitage! Did you find all the strange sights so absorbing that you couldn't drag yourself away from them?'

'I'm so *terribly* sorry I'm late,' Jenny got out.

'It would have been a little more considerate of you if you had been on time for lunch,' the Comtesse, who was assisting Simone to spoon up her grapefruit, observed in the bleakest of disapproving voices, and

Jenny felt herself colour furiously with embarrassment.

'I'm *so* sorry!' she repeated. 'I'm afraid I was having coffee with Mr. Daintry – I met him in the big square where all the little stalls are – and I didn't notice the time was passing—'

'You were doing *what*?' Célestine asked, as if the rest of the explanation had passed her by.

'Having coffee with Mr. Daintry. We went to an hotel—'

'Which hotel?'

'I think it was called the Mamounia. It was very large, and modern—'

'You'll be going there again this afternoon,' the Comtesse said, still efficiently attending to Simone, although Jenny had made an agitated move in the direction of the child and been waved away to a seat on the other side of the table, 'to take the children to see their grandmother. You'll have tea with her and her companion, and I hope you won't keep the car waiting when it arrives for you at five o'clock.' She waited for a moment to be sure that her daughter was capable of manipulating her own small silver spoon without scattering grapefruit juice over herself at the same time, and then delivered her final barbed shaft. 'And in future, when you leave this house by yourself, you will avoid having coffee, or any other form of refreshment, with masculine acquaintances who have not yet really become acquaintances, because that is something I do not care to permit,' with a dangerous flash from greenish-amber eyes. 'If you are anxious to have young men friends, we will find you some – or at least one! – but

Mr. Daintry is not to be called upon to look after my governess when she feels the need of entertainment! Is that absolutely clear?'

'I – I—' Jenny found herself stammering, half choking over her own grapefruit, and in the midst of her extreme confusion she was not even aware that a glimmering distress appeared in the eyes of the Comte as he gazed at her. But she did hear him say quickly:

'Really, my dear! I don't think Miss Armitage—'

'Miss Armitage is new to our ways here,' Célestine continued with apparent imperturbability, although her face was cold, and even the lovely scarlet line of her lips seemed touched by the forbidding coldness. 'And, for that reason, certain things must be explained to her.' She looked down the table at Jenny. 'Because you and Max are English, that is no reason why you should foregather, you know.'

Jenny felt indignation touch her, as it had touched her that morning in the presence of Max himself.

'But we met by accident – I have already explained,' she said, and felt that any further attempt to consume any more of the lunch would choke her altogether.

'Quite so,' the Comtesse murmured, 'and I am merely pointing out that it must not occur again!'

'You mean' – Jenny almost gasped – 'that if, and whenever, we meet outside this house, I am not even to acknowledge him?'

Célestine shrugged her shoulders.

'It is always possible to pass the time of day without doing more than that. And, as a matter of fact, I decided as soon as I had dropped you this morning that I should not have left you to wander about the city. You

42

are so new to this part of the world that it was hardly wise, and in future we must arrange your off-duty hours more carefully, and also the manner in which you are going to take advantage of them. In time you will get used to the fact that this country is not quite like England, or even France.'

'And, for that very reason, if I had known you proposed dropping Miss Armitage all by herself this morning I would have suggested accompanying her.' the Comte interposed. For the first time since Jenny had known him there was a strong note of displeasure in his voice. His eyes looked displeasure across the table at his wife. 'That sort of thing must not be repeated.'

'I have just said that it will not be repeated, my dear Raoul,' the Comtesse replied drawingly. 'And in any case, I made arrangements for Miss Armitage to be picked up at one o'clock by the car, but she chose to keep the chauffeur waiting.'

'A thing I'm terribly sorry about,' Jenny managed, in a small, frozen voice.

The Comte looked at her in a concerned way.

'Don't let it distress you, Miss Armitage,' he said. 'You have already apologized several times, and on the whole I think it was a very good thing you ran into Daintry this morning. I hope he showed you a few of the sights? There wasn't much time, but you probably saw something of the *suqs*, and the *medina*?'

'We – we talked,' Jenny admitted, because it was her nature to be strictly truthful.

Célestine's superb eyebrows rose.

'About England?' she inquired, with a dangerous sweetness.

43

Jenny looked at her, and then lowered her eyes swiftly.

'Yes, about England,' she concurred, again with a very great deal of truth.

'And, in the circumstances, that was, I should say, extremely natural,' the Comte murmured, and turned to decline a dish which the servant had been offering him.

Jenny had the impression – swift, and somehow rather frightening – that his wife, in the moment that his attention was concentrated elsewhere, bestowed her own full attention upon him, looking at him across the table, with its centrepiece of exotic flowers, its lace mats and its silver, and other evidences of extreme civilization. And in the look there was something which reminded her of the look in the eyes of the snake the snake-charmer had been winding about his neck in the Djemaâ el Fna that morning. At the time she had thought that the violent dislike of the snake for its charmer as expressed in those venomous bright eyes had been almost actively revolting, and now she was seeing it again in the eyes of a human being – golden-brown eyes, but just as jewel-like and brilliant.

She was glad to leave the table, and upstairs in her own room, while she got ready for the visit to the Mamounia with the children, she felt herself torn for the first time with doubts as to the wisdom of accepting such a position as this she now filled, and it was not because Max Daintry had attempted to sow seeds of doubt in her mind. The reason why he wished her to leave seemed obvious, but the fact that Célestine could behave, if she felt like it, like a feminine dictator was much more disturbing.

It prevented her from feeling any security in her job.

They were driven to the Mamounia in the big grey car. The children were very elegantly turned out, looking like the children of an American film star who were about to be brought very much into the limelight.

Simone was in a smocked dress of primrose silk, and had a straw bonnet tied under her chin with satin ribbons, while Louis had something of the air of Little Lord Fauntleroy. When they reached the hotel both children insisted on clambering out without the assistance of the chauffeur, and they swarmed into the lift ahead of both the lift attendant and Jenny, as if they were thoroughly familiar with the routine of such a visit as this, and were anxious to show off.

Their grandmother occupied a suite of rooms on the first floor, which Jenny thought must probably cost her a small fortune. And when she saw the inside of the suite, and the flowers with which it was filled, she mentally assessed the weekly bill as even higher.

The mother of the Comte, who had contracted a second marriage and was known as Lady Berringer, was a small, extremely youthful-looking person who, Jenny recognized immediately, could have been born nowhere but in England. She had fair, beautifully styled hair without a touch of grey, and her eyes were a sparkling forget-me-not blue. Her complexion was positively ravishing – and that with very little aid from cosmetics – and made Jenny think of Devonshire cream and strawberries. She was so elegantly dressed that Jenny felt instantly self-conscious about her own simple linen dress, although by comparison with the Comtesse, Lady Berringer's taste was subdued. Her dove-grey afternoon dress with its finely-pleated georgette skirt was a perfect foil for her flower-like eyes and the pale gold of her hair, and when she smiled Jenny knew at once that she was by nature friendly and spontaneous, and possibly very easy to get along with.

She welcomed the children with obvious pleasure, provided them with *bon-bons* they uninhibitedly demanded, introduced her companion, Miss Esther Harringay, who was just as unmistakably English as she was herself, and left the latter to entertain the grandchildren while she had what she described as 'a really nice little talk' with the governess.

'I've already received a glowing account of you from my son,' she said, and looked at Jenny with a faint twinkle of amusement in her bright blue eyes as the girl sat facing her on a Chesterfield. 'He said that you were not only very different from the two governesses they had before – one from France, and another, I believe, also from England – but that you were so unmistakably a lady it would be a relief to entrust the children to your care!'

'Oh!' Jenny exclaimed, and felt an embarrassed pink colour start to glow in her cheeks.

Lady Berringer smiled at her.

'It's so important, if you're going to teach them English, to pass on to them a first-class accent at the same time, and you're so young that you'll probably have lots of patience with them. Personally I find them a trifle exhausting' – Miss Harringay was at that moment being overwhelmed with requests for a game that involved a good deal of noise and rushing about, and the grandmother broke off to observe her companion giving way under the demands with a faintly rueful look in her remarkably beautiful large grey eyes – 'but that's because I'm no longer in the least young, and very set in my ways.'

Merely to look at her Jenny would have said that she couldn't be any older than somewhere in her late forties, and if her ways were 'set', they were so charmingly set that Jenny hoped secretly that hers would be exactly similar when she, too, was a grandmother.

'You, however, my dear – you're probably exactly right for them. Or you will be if you exercise a little gentle discipline. I don't believe in crushing young things.'

'Neither do I,' Jenny agreed. As a matter of fact, she and the children were already great friends, and so far she hadn't found them in the slightest degree exhausting, although they were admittedly in some ways spoiled – perhaps precocious was a better word. In others, they gave the impression that they were always rather fearful of retribution falling upon them in no mean fashion if they did anything particularly outrageous, and Jenny wondered whether it was one of the past governesses who had had methods involving stern discipline which had frightened them enough to be remembered.

Lady Berringer seemed to find it difficult to remove her eyes from Jenny's attractive, fair-skinned face and her graceful figure, and at the same time there was a faintly puzzled expression on her face.

'I was surprised that my daughter-in-law *did* insist on someone as young as you,' she admitted at last. 'Because both the other governesses were quite old, and moreover they looked like governesses. But you, very definitely, don't!'

Jenny was a little embarrassed by this sort of talk, especially in view of what had been said to her at lunch time, and she began to wonder, too, why the Comtesse de St. Alais had insisted on someone 'young' to look after her children. The answer could, of course, have been that her experience of the older ones had not been satisfactory.

Tea was brought in, and the children threatened to make themselves sick on cream cakes, and Jenny did her best to restrain them. Lady Berringer, in her amiable, good-natured way, was inclined to regard greediness as the special prerogative of the young, but the companion, who was probably not much more than thirty, although she looked older when she was not smiling, did her best to lend support to Jenny, who was anxious not only for the children's well-being but their flagrantly expensive clothes.

'Like dolls, aren't they?' their grandmother murmured, with an amused look, to Jenny. 'Célestine has the true French flair for dressing up not only herself, but her offspring.'

And in support of her employer Jenny felt forced to observe:

'But she's very, very beautiful!'

'Yes, I suppose she is,' Lady Berringer agreed, but her tone was devoid of enthusiasm.

Later she had another talk with Jenny, while the children were taken round the garden by Miss Harringay, and she asked her whether she had so far met any of her employers' friends, or made any social contacts.

'You're too young to be shut up with the children all the time,' she said. 'It simply wouldn't be fair to you, and my son wouldn't allow it, I know. Célestine will have to take you about and introduce you. You can have quite a good time out here, you know, if you wish – and, being young, you naturally couldn't wish for anything else!'

'Oh, but I'm only the governess – and I'm not in the least likely to forget that!' Jenny said quickly, and Lady Berringer smiled.

'Nonsense. You're frightfully pretty, and you're also very charming. Célestine couldn't possibly keep you hidden from her friends. But, so far, you say you've met none of them?'

'Only – Mr. Daintry,' Jenny said, and wondered why she had to pause before she brought out his name.

'Max Daintry?' the eyes of the Comte's mother widened and her slender eyebrows lifted. 'How and where did you meet him?'

Jenny explained that she had met him when he visited the house – but she did not add that there had been no one there at the time to introduce them – and Lady Berringer stared thoughtfully out of the wide-open window.

'He's an Englishman, of course – and, in a country like this, we English are apt to cling together. He's also quite a personality.'

Jenny said nothing.

Lady Berringer remarked, just before the others returned:

'So you met Max before you met anyone else out here! Well—!' She looked at Jenny curiously, and then smiled. 'But you'll meet lots and lots of young men before long. My daughter-in-law is going to be very popular with you in her house. It will be almost like having a young sister to launch socially, especially as you're really extraordinarily like her!'

CHAPTER SIX

JENNY thought of those words that night when Célestine tapped on the door of her room just before she started to dress for dinner, and asked permission to come inside.

Her manner was greatly changed since lunch time – far more friendly, in fact, than it had been hitherto. She saw that Jenny had just emerged from the bath-room, for she was wrapped in a white candlewick dressing-gown, and the ends of her hair were wet and clinging to her wide brow and the back of her slender neck.

'We're going out to dinner tonight,' Célestine said, 'and I thought you might like to come with us. As a matter of fact, as the invitation included you, I accepted on your behalf. I hope that's all right?'

'Oh – oh, yes!' Jenny answered, feeling considerably surprised. The Comtesse had absented herself every evening since her arrival, and the Comte sometimes accompanied her, but Jenny had considered this quite natural; she had not expected to be treated by them on terms of such equality that they would wish to present her in the homes of their friends. And Lady Berringer's remarks of the afternoon had struck her as unlikely to coincide with any of Célestine's own plans and intentions, at least where she herself was concerned.

But the Comtesse walked to her wardrobe and flung open the door.

'What are you going to wear?' she asked.

She ran her eye along the row of dresses, and lifted out a very pretty white muslin with sprigs of green flowers.

'This is quite suitable,' she said, 'and you should look quite nice in it. Have you a stole, or a bolero, to go with it?'

'I have a green velvet bolero,' Jenny answered.

'Then wear it. I have explained to you that the nights are chill. And I can lend you a fur wrap to wear in the car – unless, of course, you have one of your own?' with a slightly dry note in her voice.

Jenny admitted that she had nothing of the kind, and the Comtesse departed to allow her to get on with her dressing, and to wonder how she felt about the idea of wearing anything so personal as a wrap belonging to her employer, especially when the offer to wear it was made in such a cool and detached manner.

But when she went down into the hall and saw Célestine holding out to her a cloak of soft white ermine, she realized that she ought to feel grateful. Célestine herself was swathed in mink over a gown of silver lamé, and she looked absolutely striking. Beneath the flood of amber brilliance which the great swinging lantern in the hall cast upon them, as they stood congregated in the middle of a glorious Bokhara carpet, Jenny had no idea that she herself, in the filmy white dress that made her look very young indeed, and the green bolero that did such attractive things to her hair, with its autumn gold colouring, made a picture calculated to attract any eye that was not deliberately fastened to something else.

And the eye of the Comte de St. Alais rested upon her with unconcealed admiration when she arrived at the foot of the stairs.

His wife, as if she was approving some goods she had just ordered to be sent home, said:

'You look extremely nice. You have good taste.'

And then they were outside in the car, and the Comte himself was at the wheel, while Jenny – although she was not quite certain how the arrangement came about – was seated beside him, and Célestine sat enthroned on the back seat in a kind of solitary grandeur.

The night was very dark, but there were brilliant stars away up in the deep night sky. Jenny had not thought it the correct thing to display sufficient curiosity to ask where they were going, and who were the people she was likely to meet that night, but once they had crossed the Djemaâ el Fna, where kerosene lamps lighted the various stalls and the open-sided tents, and there appeared to be as much excitement and movement as there was in the daytime, they turned in the direction of the French town at the end of a long avenue of palm trees. The avenue was also bordered by orange trees – the golden badge of Marrakesh – but Jenny was unable to recognize these under the purple canopy of night.

When they arrived at their destination there were already several cars drawn up in the short drive which led to the large white modern house, with lights flaming from every window.

In the blaze of light Jenny caught a glimpse of the inevitable fountain, and a solid wall of crimson and

53

purple bougainvillea, as well as some bushes of red camellias, and trails of purple convolvulus.

Inside the house the furnishings were luxurious in the extreme, and the shaded lights cast over everything a romantic shimmer. Her host and hostess proved to be a Captain Benoît and his wife, and there were so many other guests that, although Madame Benoît singled out Jenny for a little smiling conversation before drinks were handed round, she had to leave her very quickly and pay similar attention to others, and Jenny was left with an excellent opportuniy to take stock of her attractive surroundings.

But just before they went to dinner Célestine herself brought a young man up to introduce to her, and although his eyes were mysteriously dark, his hair was so strikingly golden that she received quite a shock of surprise when the Comtesse presented him as Si Mohammed Menebhi. He had beautiful manners, and his French was quite effortless, but his English was much more halting. He wore a white shell jacket and black cummerbund, and his eyelashes were the longest she had ever seen in her life, and lent to his lustrous eyes a touch of something vaguely disturbing.

At dinner Si Mohammed sat at her right hand, and Jenny found his conversation so interesting, although it had to be carried on chiefly in French, that it was not until several courses had been served that she found herself looking down the length of the table and straight into the eyes of Max Daintry.

There was a mocking, amused look in those eyes, but the set of his mouth and jaw was a little grim, she thought, especially when his glance shifted for an instant to Si Mohammed. The latter acknowledged him with a faintly arrogant inclination of the head, and then continued his conversation with Jenny, as if he was not aware that for one moment, at least, she had been quite noticeably and considerably taken aback by the suddenly discovered presence of the other man.

'Tell me,' said the golden-headed Moor, 'how long you are thinking of staying in Marrakesh, Miss Armitage?' His ardent eyes said that he hoped the stay was likely to be a protracted one. 'And tell me also how you like it here.'

'Oh, I like it very much,' she admitted, quite truthfully – although there were certain aspects of the Morocco she had seen so far which repelled her. The poverty that dwelt side by side with the brightness of the colour, and the golden warmth of the sun. The barbarism which lurked so near the surface, and which had frightened her in the market-place, when she had watched the snake-charmer and the medicine-men. But the beauty of the High Atlas, the green beauty of the carefully irrigated oasis outside the rose-red walls of the city, which even in the burning desert summer was fresh and green – or so she had been given to understand – and the noble, twelfth-century beauty of the Koutoubiya mosque, in its garden of cypresses, which the Comtesse had driven her to see one afternoon, were things she would never forget.

'And you *are* going to remain amongst us for perhaps a very long while?'

'That depends on the amount of satisfaction I give to my employers, the Comte and Comtesse de St. Alais,' she answered, and was aware that Max Daintry, although he, too, was engaged in conversation with his neighbour – who was *not* Célestine, at that moment looking rather bored because her nearest neighbour was a stout and very elderly Frenchman, riding his favourite hobby-horse which was French politics – was still looking down the table towards her, and that he appeared to be observing her every movement with detached interest.

'Then, in that case, it is almost certain you will remain,' Si Mohammed declared, triumphantly.

'Why?' she asked, looking at him smilingly – and if the smile was rather brilliant, and perhaps just a shade provocative, that was for the benefit of Max Daintry.

'Why?' the young Moor echoed. 'Because it is obvious that you could never be anything other than a success, and you are bound to give satisfaction!'

Jenny decided that perhaps the smile had been a little too brilliant, and tried to change the subject by introducing as an alternative the various places of interest to be visited locally.

'How much have you seen?' he asked. 'The *medina*, of course, and the *suqs*—? But how much of what lies beyond?'

'Why, nothing,' Jenny had to admit. 'But then I've been here such a short while, haven't I?'

'Then, in that case, I must show it all to you! Madame la Comtesse will give me permission, and I will drive you wherever you wish to be driven.' He sounded extremely enthusiastic, and instead of being completely dark his eyes all at once discovered an amber light in them which caressed her, and his features were so perfectly chiselled and so absolutely fault-less that, but for the fact that whenever she looked sideways at him he instantly seized the opportunity to look sideways at her, she would have enjoyed studying them in a leisurely fashion, just as she might have been tempted to study a piece of sculpture. 'My father has a house in the High Atlas, and perhaps one day, if we can persuade the Comtesse to accompany you, you will pay him a visit?'

Jenny managed to evade this question, and others similar to it, and she was not at all sorry when the long-drawn-out meal ended, and the diners all dispersed and formed fresh groups. Si Mohammed would have clung determinedly to her, but she managed to evade him by escaping to the hostess's bedroom, which was being used as a ladies' cloakroom, and having effected a few repairs to her make-up she wrapped the Com-tesse's cloak around her and made up her mind to have a quick look at the garden in the light of the moon which had now risen.

She was standing like a slim, white, petrified figure, utterly entranced by the magic of moonlight on mosaic paths and beds of flowers that filled the night with exciting and disturbing perfume, while around her rose silvered walls and motionless palms, and the distant gleaming white range of the Atlas mountains, when a voice spoke to her – and once again it was from behind!

'Why do you always put yourself into the sort of position which makes it necessary for me to creep up on you?' Daintry asked, and she knew he was smoking a Turkish cigarette, because the fragrance of it reached her above the fragrance of the flowers before ever she turned to look at him.

He gave her a half mocking, half formal, bow.

'How enchanting you look tonight,' he said. 'But no doubt Si Mohammed has already told you much the same thing? I noticed you were getting along very well at dinner.'

Jenny ignored this observation, but she said quietly:

'I thought you were annoyed with me this morning – much too annoyed to speak to me tonight!'

'Not at all,' he assured her in a casual, leisurely manner. 'I put to you a suggestion, and you preferred to think I had some sort of an ulterior motive, so we'll forget the whole thing, shall we?' He slipped two fingers beneath her elbow and propelled her forward along the path, and she found herself moving as if compelled at his side. 'You don't get this sort of night in England, do you? At least, not if my memory serves me rightly, for it's a good many years now since I visited my own homeland. Not that I have as much right to call it my homeland as you have, because my mother was the daughter of a Roman surgeon, and that makes me half Italian, doesn't it? And as I choose to live in Morocco that makes me something of a mongrel – or at least, I'm sure you think so!'

'I don't!' Jenny denied, almost too hastily. And then she added: 'But it does explain—' And then she broke off.

'What?' he asked, as if he was interested.

'Nothing,' she said, rather feebly, because if she told him that the fact that he was not wholly English helped to explain that unusual swarthiness of his, and the kind of grey eyes she had never seen before in her life, he would probably be highly amused.

'Which means you'd rather not tell me?'

'There's nothing to tell.'

'I see,' he murmured, and looked down at her with the smile in his eyes which told her that he was amused. He touched the collar of her cloak. 'Are you quite sure you're warm enough, or would you rather go back to the house?'

'No – no, I like it out here.'

'And if we keep moving you're hardly likely to catch a chill.' He stopped for a moment beside a white painted seat to offer her a cigarette, and after a moment's hesitation she selected one. 'Virginia on the right, and Turkish on the left,' he directed her. 'Better not risk the Turkish, because they'd be much too strong for a little girl like you.'

'I wish you wouldn't call me a little girl,' she said impatiently.

'Why not?' he asked. 'You're certainly not a big one, are you?'

As she looked up at him, and he held his lighter to the tip of her cigarette, she thought that the smile on his mouth was indulgent, but his eyes had as much mockery in them as always. Apart from that he seemed to her to be immensely tall, and his shoulders were very well held, and with just the right amount of breadth, under his white dinner-jacket.

'Was the Comtesse annoyed with you because you were late this morning?' he asked, as they moved on.

'Yes.' She looked up at him quickly, in surprise. 'And she was also annoyed because — because I met you!'

'Dear me!' he murmured, but showed no surprise. 'Then she'd hardly approve of our walking out here tonight, would she?'

Jenny felt almost repelled by his words, and moved a little away from him. He was too smooth, too casual, too indifferent, apparently, to anyone's feelings but his own — and they were of such a superficial order that he could probably control them at will! Or that was what she told herself. She looked sideways at him, with a touch of scorn.

'Why did you really ask me to go home this morning? What is your *real* reason for wanting me to go?'

'I haven't any reason,' he replied composedly, 'and I have no desire for you to go, either. So we won't discuss it any more, will we? We'll just forget it.'

'But you *wanted* me to go,' she reminded him. 'You were quite urgent about it.'

He shrugged his shoulders. His eyes, as he looked down at her, were suddenly veiled, and he turned her about so that they faced back to the house.

'Nevertheless, we'll forget it. And instead I'd like to hear the truth about how you and Célestine get on,'

'Oh, quite well.'

'I've known Célestine for years,' he said. 'She was a model in Paris when first we came across one another, but she's gone quite a way since then. She succeeded in marrying very well, and I'm sure you'll agree that the Comte is all a woman could desire in a husband?'

She answered carefully:

'I hardly know him, but he seems very nice – and kind!'

'And in your opinion kindness is very important in a husband?'

She looked at him suspiciously.

'Do you really want to know my opinion?'

'Oh, yes,' he answered. 'Because I feel sure that the man you marry will not only have to ooze kindness, but he'll also have to be someone very young and pure, straight out of a theological college. He'll never have kissed a woman in his life – not even on the top of the head! – and as for having kissed the head of a *married* woman—!'

She knew that he was mocking her, and drew even farther away from him, so that he was forced to drop her arm, and fortunately the path was wide enough to permit a foot of space between them. He could feel her looking at him with strengthened suspicion, and as he looked down at her and saw that her small face was touched by moonlight he smiled at her suddenly.

'What a pretty child you are!' he exclaimed, and she felt the compliment was most inappropriate.

The distance between them and the house lessened. He remarked conversationally:

'Wouldn't you like to know something about how, and why, I come to be mixed up with the St. Alais?' As she did not answer, he went on: 'As a matter of fact, the Comte and I collect pictures together, and not only pictures but fine furniture, and books, and all sorts of *objets d'art* from all over the world. And then, of course, we sell them again sometimes, in order to make a profit. And as a side-line I do a little gun-running and dope-smuggling, and so forth — which is also profitable!' As he saw her eyes widen in horror he laughed dryly. 'Well, you've already assigned me the role of a home-wrecker, haven't you? And there's no reason why you should stop there! For all you know to the contrary, I may have all sorts of potentialities and possibilities — some of them unknown even to myself!'

She felt herself flushing brilliantly in the moonlight, but this time there was nothing soft in his eyes, and they had no sympathy in them, either.

'Do you generally make up your mind about people you meet before you have a chance to check on them?'

Her colour burned more deeply into her cheeks.

'Well, you must admit, it did look a little — a little odd,' she defended herself. 'You kissed me — a perfect stranger! — and you didn't even attempt to make sure I was not a stranger! And, even so—'

'Even so, Célestine is a married woman, and you're very full of sympathy for the Comte, aren't you? Well, we'll leave *that* at that, shall we?'

They were now almost back to the house, but she had a chance to study him more carefully before the moonlit garden was left behind. Certainly that noticeable jaw of his was not indicative of weakness, and there was not much sign of it in the unrelenting line of his lips, either. And although his eyes derided, and were frequently inscrutable, they were capable of long, hard looks, and were not the kind of eyes to look hurriedly away. In fact, she could not imagine him under any circumstances yielding ground of any sort to another, and in a battle of wills his would be the stronger — at any rate, so far as she herself was concerned, for when he looked directly at her she *had* to look away, and she was a little afraid of that strange compelling *something* which was a part of his personality. As, for instance, when he had coolly taken her arm and led her away down the garden — although he had parted from her without even a curt 'good-bye' only that morning!

Just before they passed through the enclosed patio back into the brightly-lighted house he paused abruptly and asked:

'What was it you said about Célestine being annoyed because you met me this morning?'

Jenny, too, paused, and looked up at him gravely, although her eyes watched him carefully while she answered.

'She said you were so slight an acquaintance it was not correct for me to do anything more than merely acknowledge you if I met you outside the house. And that in future I am not to do anything more than that.'

His black brows drew more closely together, and she thought that for an instant a hard expression flashed into his eyes. And then he looked down at her in that strange, inscrutable way he had, and said almost curtly,

'I wouldn't let that curb upon your own inclinations upset you, if I were you, although I've no doubt the Comtesse is thinking merely of you, and the fact that she is in a sense responsible for you while you are a member of her household. But if she suggests that you see no more of Si Mohammed Menebhi I would follow her advice to the letter!'

But, as it was the Comtesse herself who had made a deliberate point of introducing the extraordinarily handsome Moor to her new, young, and perhaps dangerously impressionable governess, Jenny did not feel, somehow, that any such prohibition would be laid upon her.

'Don't worry about Célestine,' Daintry remarked suddenly, looking down at her. 'And as I am – or, at least, a part of me is – a fellow countryman of yours, there's no reason why I shouldn't show you the sights of Marrakesh if you'd care to be shown them by me. When are you due for another break from nursery duties?'

'I don't know,' Jenny admitted. 'The Comtesse said she was going to go into the matter of my off-duty times, and arrange various things that I could do – with her approval – when I was free.'

'I see,' he said slowly. She thought, for an instant, a spark of humour appeared in his eyes. 'Then in that case I shall have to apply to her for permission to remove you from the safety of the St. Alais nest, won't I?'

'And you'll do that?' she asked, with so much unmistakable surprise in her eyes that his old, mocking smile appeared on his lips.

'Oh yes, I'll do that! I even entered a lion's cage once, when the trainer was absent, without being badly mauled! And I'm not really afraid of Célestine, you know!'

She knew that his voice was mocking her, as well as his look, but the surprise remained strong within her.

He was right when he said she had made up her mind about him — and it was not the simplest matter in the world to un-make it. Besides, there had been Célestine's behaviour at lunch time.

'If Célestine gives permission, are you likely to withhold your own acceptance of an invitation from me to see some of the local sights in my company?'

Dance music, soft and seductive, was stealing out to them from the open windows and doors of the house, and they could see couples swaying gracefully beneath the discreetly shaded lights. There were one or two smart French uniforms, and some breathtakingly lovely frocks. And from behind them the peculiarly pungent scent of the lily-tree, which flowers all over Morocco, reached them, and there was the plash of incessantly falling water into a marble basin. Jenny looked upwards at the huge stars that were wheeling above them in a violet sky, and at the astonishingly pure light of the moon — such moonlight she had never seen before, and it was making a wonder of Marrakesh, with its minarets and its palms and its rose-red walls. She felt for a moment that she was very, very far from home, and lowering her glance to the dark, but completely strong face of the man who stood beside her she found herself answering with just the merest touch of hesitation in her voice — so that it sounded more like a catch of her breath:

'No — no, I don't think so . . .'

He laughed suddenly, and very softly. And to her surprise he reached out and caught her hand, giving it such a hard, almost convulsive squeeze that she felt her fingers tingling as a result of it for quite a long time afterwards.

'Brave girl!' he exclaimed, and although there was undoubted mockery in his voice, it was very gentle mockery this time, and somehow she didn't mind. She didn't even mind that hard squeeze of her fingers, and as they went up the steps side by side and back into the over-heated crush of the house she didn't greatly care that Célestine saw them.

CHAPTER SEVEN

SOMEWHAT to Jenny's surprise Célestine said nothing to her afterwards about her emergence from the garden with Max Daintry, and she was particularly pleasant on the drive home. She did say, however – and this made Jenny feel, although she could not quite explain the sensation to herself, or why she should even feel it, as if someone had ruffled her back hair up the wrong way – that Si Mohammed Menebhi had found her so charming that he had had to admit as much to Célestine herself. In fact, he was quite bowled over by Jenny, as he was a very rich young man, and many young women found him attractive, this was most decidedly a compliment which even Jenny – who no doubt prided herself on being English! – could regard as a feather in her cap.

'The Menebhi family is a very old family,' Célestine observed, as if she was determined to drive home to Jenny the significance of any member of it singling her out for approving comment. 'And Si Mohammed is not merely good-looking, he is quite sensational!'

Jenny said nothing, and the Comte, at the wheel, sent her a sudden sideways look which, although it was too dark for her to be able to read easily the expression in his eyes, provided her with the strong feeling that he was sending out to her waves of sympathetic understanding because he sensed that inside her she was shrinking with a kind of repugnance from his wife's line of conversation.

'Apart from anything else, I hope you had a good evening?' he asked in his gentle voice, and recalling those moments in the garden, with the magic of moonlight all about her, and the heavy scent of flowers in the air, and Max Daintry looking at her out of those strange, smoky-grey eyes of his, she was able to answer honestly that she had. For now there was something like a truce between her and Daintry, and she could not forget that in a moment of feeling lost and far from home the grip of his fingers had been curiously comforting.

When they reached home the Comte invited Jenny to join them for a drink in the big main *salon,* and as Célestine appeared to be in a very amiable mood the girl felt it was safe to accept. She found herself wondering why the Comtesse's mood was so unusually mellow, for not once during the evening had Jenny observed her have any conversation alone with Max — although, of course, it was possible that they had managed to contrive this while she was not looking — and when Jenny and Max had reappeared from the garden and Célestine had met them there had, for an instant, been a very hard look in her eyes.

But now she appeared secretly very well satisfied about something, and lay back in a very elegant attitude on a satin-covered Empire couch, and studied Jenny almost complacently. The Comte brought them both drinks, looking very slender and distinguished in his evening things, and Jenny was impressed as always by the beauty of the room in which they sat. It contained so much that was costly and rare — so many

68

examples of priceless furniture, pictures and ornaments. The rugs were rich and rare, the lights shone
softly across them so that none of the beauty was
missed. And flowers were massed in great bowls of
beaten copper and silver, and there was even one richly
chased golden bowl which held some of the lilies that
smelled as if they were drenched with exotic incense.

Jenny looked at the Comtesse, in her silver lamé
dress, with her flaming hair and her perfect face, and
she recalled that Max Daintry had told her that this
beautiful wife of the Comte had once been a Paris
model. And she was not in the least surprised, for
clothes worn by her acquired an elegance and a perfection beyond the dreams even of the designers, and a
sack worn by her would probably have appeared to
greater advantage than an exclusively designed model
on many another woman.

But, despite the beauty and the seemingly effortless
grace, there was something in the cool, chiselled lines of
the face which, Jenny knew, could repel. There was
something hard and intolerant, and impatient of any of
the softening influences, which could have provided a
clue to the type of life she had led before she was fortunate enough to marry the Comte de St. Alais. And if
that clue was not entirely misleading Raoul de St. Alais
had lifted her above an existence where struggle and
hardship had not been unknown, and memories of the
hardships were not easily banished.

That was why, perhaps, when she looked at the vic-
arage-bred Jenny, whose life until the death of her
father had been uneventful and monotonous and
devoid of all glamour, and any form of real excitement,

her lovely lips curled, and a gleam of contempt appeared in her eyes. Jenny had been protected all her life, and if she was alone and unprotected now that did not awaken any deep feeling of sympathy in the Parisienne's heart.

That was one reason why every time she looked at her husband her look expressed contempt, for he had known luxury all his life, and was still knowing it, and in spite of all that he had given her she despised him for it.

Jenny felt — and hoped that perhaps she was wrong — that if Madame la Comtesse de St. Alais had lived at the time of the French Revolution she would have been overwhelmingly on the side of the revolutionaries, and when members of her husband's family lost their heads beneath the 'kiss' of the guillotine she would probably have applauded enthusiastically.

The Comte came across to Jenny and sat beside her on another of the little Empire couches, and he asked her interested questions about her home life in England, and the kind of things she was interested in. When Jenny admitted how uneventful her life had been, and how simple were her tastes, she could feel, rather than see, Célestine's heavy white eyelids drooping disdainfully, and the curl of the scarlet lips was almost openly sneering.

At last, as if she deemed it time for Jenny to learn that she was still only someone who could be dismissed and summoned at will, in spite of the Comte's attentiveness, she said:

'You'd better go to bed, my dear, otherwise you won't be very fresh in the morning. And you certainly won't be able to keep pace with the freshness of the children.'

Jenny stood up, covered in confusion, and afraid that she must have appeared to be taking advantage of favours shown to her in her humble position as a governess. But the Comte's eyes were very kind as he bade her good night, and his hand held hers strongly when she gave it to him. For one instant, as she felt the close grip of his fingers, she remembered the grip of those other fingers that had held hers, and then escaped somewhat hastily from the room.

In the morning, she made a point of being up early in order that no one could accuse her of neglecting her duties, and although the children were certainly very fresh they were not too fresh for her to cope with. For one thing, in the short time that she had known them she had succeeded in winning their hearts completely, and although they were not the most tractable of children, towards her at least they were never openly rebellious, although the unfortunate Nerida often found them so.

In the afternoon they went for a drive, and as they were gliding smoothly along one of the narrow lanes of the *medina*, with high walls shutting out the sunshine, and cascades of blossom providing a kind of canopy for the car to pass beneath, the chauffeur was forced hastily to apply his brakes when out through an open doorway rode an unforgettable figure on a pure white horse with a long, flowing tail.

The car was open, and the children clutched eagerly at the sides to watch the horseman gain sufficient control of his mount to turn him in the narrow street.

There was a wild clattering of hoofs, the gleam of silver spurs, and Si Mohammed Menebhi ranged himself and his superb mount along one side of the car, and looked down at Jenny, where she sat between her two charges on the dove-grey velvet seat.

He was wearing white riding-breeches and high polished boots, a jacket of fine white drill, and a long cloak lined with scarlet which was flung back over his shoulders and streamed out behind him like a flaunting banner. On his amazingly golden head was set a low *tarboosh*, and out of the delicate olive of his face his large, extraordinarily beautiful dark eyes gazed at Jenny with open admiration. She saw his teeth flash whitely as he smiled.

'What a delightful encounter, Miss Armitage!' he exclaimed. 'Is this a customary afternoon airing? Because, if so, I shall look out for you more often!'

Jenny was so taken aback by his unexpected appearance that she found it difficult to formulate an immediate and suitable reply, but he seemed quite content merely to smile at her, while the children gazed up at him open-mouthed. Jenny was wearing an ice-blue dress of crisp linen, with a white belt and sandals, and her hair was partly concealed beneath a wide-brimmed hat that was white too. In the shade of the high walls, her skin looked remarkably fair, and her eyes large and deep like shadowy purple pansies.

Si Mohammed Menebhi bent lower in his saddle and addressed her softly:

'The Comtesse has given me permission to call upon you and take you out, Miss Armitage, when you have free time. I am very impatient to take you out, so will you not tell me when you are likely to be free?'

'I really haven't any idea at the moment,' Jenny answered, scarcely hoping that he would believe her. 'But it is very kind of you,' she added.

'There is no kindness in doing something one can barely wait to do.' His eyes, with the curious, lambent lights in them like golden flames leaping up and down, remained fixed on her face, and the tiny smile on his mouth reminded her of the smile on the lips of the Sphinx. 'When, Miss Armitage? When may I call?'

'I – I really don't know—' Jenny stammered.

'Tomorrow afternoon? I will take you to tea where there is dancing and music. Or perhaps tomorrow night you will dine with me? It is not necessary that you look after these children at night time!' with a not very approving glance at them.

But Jenny shook her head, and she managed to make it a firm shake.

'I shall have to ask the Comtesse. I really must consult her before I make any plans whatsoever, so although it is very kind of you . . .' She didn't know what else to say, but although the tiny smile vanished from his lips his eyes remained soft and caressing.

His horse started to become impatient, and he had some little difficulty in controlling it in the narrow space. But he was obviously a magnificent horseman, and Jenny could not help but admire the way he finally succeeded in quieting the impatient animal, remaining at the same time completely cool and undisturbed.

The chauffeur was waiting with his foot hovering over the brake, and Jenny leaned forward and addressed him. Then she looked upwards at Si Mohammed and smiled at him.

'I can be patient,' he assured her, and with a slight inclination of the head, but ignoring the children altogether, he gave the fretting horse its head and swept past the car, and the three occupants of the back seat watched him disappearing in a small cloud of dust which unfortunately settled all over them.

When they reached home Jenny did not tell the Comtesse about her encounter with the Moor, and in fact she did not see her for the rest of that day. But the following morning Célestine sent for Jenny to attend upon her in her own room, and when the governess entered she found Célestine still lying comfortably relaxed in bed – an enormous French bed quilted in amber satin, and with an amber satin coverlet – and looking exquisite in a completely transparent nightdress of pale green chiffon with narrow black velvet ribbons running through it, and a black lace bed-jacket round her shoulders. Her hair flamed over her silk-covered pillows.

'I have something to tell you which might, or might not, interest you,' she said. Her golden eyes studied Jenny obliquely, and her white eyelids looked heavy, as if they were still languid and weighted with sleep. 'Max Daintry asked me last night whether he could take you out tomorrow to show you Marrakesh. It is natural—' her tone became rather noticeably drawling – 'that being a fellow countryman of yours he should sympathize with your feeling of strangeness among so many foreigners, and as the children have taken to you so well, and I wish you to settle down here, I think it a good plan. Have you any objections to raise to it yourself? You would not, perhaps prefer to have lunch with Si Mohammed Menebhi, who is also pleading for your favours?' with a good deal of dryness.

'I—why, I—' Jenny stammered, when her employer interrupted her.

'Don't bother to appear embarrassed. You are young and pretty, and naturally the men will notice you. But Max is quite safe, and no one knows Marrakesh better than he does, so you will no doubt enjoy it in his company. And Si Mohammed will lose none of his enthusiasm by being forced to wait a little.' Her eyes slid over Jenny as if the girl and the situation amused her.

Jenny finally left the room to return to her charges with the bewildered feeling that her whole life was being organized for her just then. It was not what she really wished to do – it was what the Comtesse decided she should do! And for some reason, in spite of all she had previously said, she had no objection to Jenny's spending several hours in the company of Max Daintry.

Max had seen the Comtesse the night before! And he had managed to persuade her that it was a good thing for him to take Jenny out! . . .

CHAPTER EIGHT

Jenny was called for about eleven o'clock the following morning by Daintry with his car, and within a short time after that the car was parked and they were exploring on foot the narrow labyrinth of the *medina* and the *suqs* wherein she had not previously had an opportunity to set foot. With her tall companion preventing her from being jostled by burly Arabs and laden donkeys, Riff women with straw hats descending almost to their shoulders, and whining beggars who occasionally sought to block their path, Jenny moved for the first time freely, and with wide eyes, amongst such a heterogeneous press of people that she realized that her comparatively sheltered life in England had not prepared her for such sights.

The crowd wound like a colourful snake between the whitewashed houses and ochre-coloured walls, and the air was heavy with the smell of charcoal fires, sandalwood, drying foods, jasmine and attar of roses. There were shops full of leather goods, copper and brassware shops, weavers' shops, and shops where the colourful Moorish slippers were displayed in quantities. Other shops displayed silk scarves and European clothes, but to Jenny they had a look of shoddiness which was unattractive, and she was dismayed by dark and dismal interiors which to her were more than a little forbidding. But for the blue sky overhead, and the brilliant sunshine that occasionally found its way into even the meanest alley, there would have been little to tempt her to linger, even had her escort permitted her to do so. And so far as he was concerned she had the impression that he had done this sort of thing so many times before that any novelty it might once have possessed had long since evaporated.

She much preferred it when they returned to the car and he drove her down the long avenue which led to the French town, and pointed out to her public gardens ablaze with flowers, golden orange groves, the Palace of the Pasha, and the slender towers of minarets. In the course of that morning's outing she saw more of the French town than she had ever seen before, the Minara gardens with their artificial lake and pavilion – to which, Daintry told her, with an odd smile on his lips, a Sultan of the past used to retire with his reigning favourite, whom he eventually drowned in the lake – and the great gateway of Marrakesh, the Bab Aguenaou.

On the whole, Jenny found her escort knowledge-able, patient, understanding of the sort of things she would like to see, and those she would prefer to avoid – and when she suddenly clutched at his arm in one of the *suqs* and uttered an exclamation of horror because a half-starved cat robbed of its ears by disease darted between her legs, or a blind beggar with fearsome eye-sockets appeared in her path, he knew that things of that sort appalled her.

'You're too sensitive,' he said to her, rather harshly, when he felt her fingers clinging to his sleeve. 'Or perhaps you have been too carefully brought up,' with a great deal of dryness.

'I couldn't bear to live in a place like this, surrounded by these things, and do nothing about them,' she told him.

'In that case,' he said, 'and if all people felt like you, nothing would be done about them,' and she decided that that was very definitely a rebuke.

Shortly before one o'clock, therefore, when he told her that he was taking her to lunch, she was not much surprised to find that they were returning to the *medina*. The French part of the town, she felt somehow certain, had little attraction for him, and in the *medina* it had struck her that he was very well known. Some faces had actually brightened when he passed by, and smiles and glances at him were all smiles and glances of approval.

What did surprise her was the type of place he had chosen for lunch. It was in a particularly narrow lane, and a low door admitted them to very much the same sort of patio that fronted the entrance to the St. Alais house, which also was in the oldest part of the town, and possibly one of the oldest houses in it. But the house Jenny suddenly saw standing in front of her, hidden away from the encroaching outside world by the usual high and unscaleable wall, was small, white and modern, with a flat roof and trailing creepers trained to conceal the bareness of the walls, and a garden full of colour surrounding it on three sides.

Jenny looked so surprised that Daintry gazed down at her with an amused look.

'I hope you don't feel that it's improper to have lunch alone with a bachelor like myself in his own house, but I decided that you would probably enjoy the meal more here, and the Mamounia has unpleasing associations which I thought you'd rather forget.'

As Jenny entered the big main living-room of the house, access to which was gained from the patio, she looked up at him.

'*Your* house?'

'Yes, mine!'

'And you live here – all alone?'

'All alone apart from my one or two excellent servants, yes. Why?' His glance down at her now was definitely mocking. 'Do you feel very much alarmed?'

'Of course not!' she exclaimed, and felt herself flushing brilliantly. Why she had made that absurd remark about his living there all alone she couldn't think, because naturally, if the house was his own, and as he was a bachelor, he lived there alone. And hard on the heels of his own mocking inquiry came the remembrance of words Célestine had used about him the morning before: 'Max is quite safe! . . .'

Why had Célestine thought it was necessary to tell her that Max was quite safe? And what, in any case, had she meant by it?

Jenny tried not to be aware of the man standing close to her as she looked about her at the cool and pleasant place in which she found herself after her morning's sight-seeing. It was beautifully furnished after a somewhat severe fashion, and apart from some comfortable modern armchairs and a cocktail cabinet in a corner, here, just as in the St. Alais house, there were some valuable period pieces. The floor of black and white tiles was strewn with glowing Persian rugs,

79

and in an alcove stood a beautiful bronze figure of a Negro boy. There was a Chinese lacquer cabinet and matching low tables, a standard lamp upheld by another graceful bronze, and heavy silk curtains flowing beneath the arch which led to an adjoining dining-room.

Jenny was impressed by the excessive orderliness, and the somewhat restrained taste which prevailed. There were few cushions, no ornaments – or rather, knick-knacks – which was perhaps not surprising, and there was a monastic atmosphere of peacefulness which Jenny found extremely pleasing after the heat and the glare and the discord outside.

Max indicated a settee, and automatically she removed her hat and sat down. Her soft gold tendrils of hair were clinging moistly to her brow, and when he had brought her a drink her host – who, all at once, had become the urbane and perfectly polished host without any mockery in either his look or his voice – suggested that she might like to withdraw to a dressing-room on the ground floor and refresh herself with a wash, and of course, a re-application of make-up before lunch. She was only too glad to take advantage of this offer, feeling sticky and almost dirty after the squalor of the *suqs*, and when she saw the beautiful tiled bathroom which adjoined the admirably equipped dressing-room she was delighted that she had done so.

When she rejoined him, she was conscious of appearing to much more advantage, particularly as her dress of hedge-rose pink, with the wide white collar and belt she favoured so much, was new and most becoming, and her hair was shining like a polished chestnut.

Max Daintry provided her with another drink, and they sat for a while talking in a relaxed fashion on the subject of some of the sights she had seen that morning. Then a servant announced that lunch was ready to be served and they moved to the dining-room, which was all very light, with light wood furniture, and an outlook over beds of brilliant flowers. Jenny decided she liked this smaller house better than the St. Alais's, for in some ways it reminded her of a modern villa at home in England, although not many English villas were as lavishly equipped.

Daintry remarked her absorption with the outlook, and with the artistic arrangement of flowers on the table, and he asked her at last – with a hint of dryness in his tone again:

'You like my house, and my way of living? Or am I, perhaps, getting the wrong impression altogether?'

'Oh, no.' She looked at him with a quick, almost eager, smile, which lighted up her face and made her eyes acquire a new depth of colour. 'I think it's delightful, and I also think for a bachelor you are exceedingly comfortable.'

'Why for a bachelor?' he asked, one of his dark eyebrows lifting. 'And how,' shattering her composure, 'do you know that I am a bachelor?'

'I don't! At least' – flushing in the fashion over which she had so little control – 'I only assumed . . .'

'Well, as a matter of fact,' he answered with a cool smile, 'your assumption is entirely correct. I am a bachelor, and probably likely to remain one – but that's because I enjoy the comforts you seem to imagine are the prerogative only of a married man! Whereas, in point of fact, a married man's household ceases to hold much comfort for him, and it is the woman who almost certainly gets most out of marriage for the reason that she usually runs her home as she likes. Never – or very seldom! – as her husband likes!'

'I see,' Jenny said, feeling that by making such a statement he had flung down a challenge – almost certainly quite deliberate – and that the friendly comradeship which had seemed to exist between them during the morning had all at once, and very abruptly, flown away out of the window. She felt it was no longer possible to meet his eyes directly, and stared at the centrepiece of deep purple flowers. 'Then, in that case, it's certainly safer for you to remain a bachelor, isn't it?'

'I've no intention of doing otherwise!'

She felt her neck growing painfully hot.

'Though that, of course, is rather a selfish attitude.'

'Is it? I'm afraid I'm not concerned with how my attitude strikes other people.'

'I see,' she said again, and as they had reached the coffee stage of the meal, and he had just poured her a liqueur, she took a hasty sip at it, although she disliked liqueurs extremely.

'But naturally,' he remarked, sitting back in his chair and regarding her with unconcealed amusement, 'being a young woman for whom nothing short of marriage was obviously intended, you would deplore what you are pleased to look upon as selfishness! Wasted material, shall we say, since there are so many more women in the world than men?'

She forced herself to look at him with a touch of grave consideration.

'I don't think that aspect of the matter is really important,' she replied, 'if the material is not likely to prove suitable for marriage. And on your own admission you have a sort of antipathy towards it.'

'Not an antipathy – I feel safer as I am!'

'And as there are already so many unhappy marriages' – thinking of Célestine and Raoul de St. Alais, and in particular Raoul's look of silently enduring a good deal, which brought a faint shadow to her eyes – 'you are wise not to add to them. Very wise, I should say!'

'Indeed,' he murmured. 'And what are the essential qualifications for marriage, perhaps you can tell me?'

She shook her head slowly.

'I don't know. But a determination to make it work out successfully would be one of them, I should think.'

'You're wiser than I thought you were,' he commented. 'Anything else?'

'An overwhelming desire for it in the first place,' she said. 'That's surely the most important?'

He looked at her with a kind of cool approval.

'An overwhelming desire for anything almost always results in one making a tremendous effort to obtain it. How right you are! But by the same token my blood must flow very sluggishly, for I have never felt that overwhelming urge! And you are too young to have done so – yet!'

She felt that the conversation had become acutely

embarrassing, and wished she could think of something to say to divert it. But in his company she was not very good at thinking of conversational openings, and she was glad to hear him say suddenly:

'Tell me something about yourself – your life in England. I know it can't have been very exciting,' with a sudden, half humorous look in his eyes, 'at least, not judged by the standards of anyone like – say Célestine! But even so it's probably had its highlights. Has it?'

She shook her head again, but she gave him a brief word picture of the kind of life she had led since the death of her father, when her home was sold, and there was nothing very much from the proceeds except to defray expenses and debts. And she had had one job as a nursery governess, which had not worked out very well because her employer had really wanted a domestic help as well, and the job had been rather a heavy one. And it had not, in any case, been a happy one.

'And so you decided to come to Morocco,' he said, 'in search of happiness?'

'No; merely because it was the most suitable job that was offered me, and there were no ties to keep me in England.'

'And that brings us back to the advantages of marriage if one wishes to develop ties!' He smiled at her rather oddly, and then noticed that she looked a shade rebellious. She could not get away from the feeling that he was mocking her deliberately all the time, and wondered whether it was because she had ventured to form her own opinion of him without, as he had said, attempting to check her facts first! In short she had been ready to condemn him from the very word go – but not without a measure of good cause. In fact, quite a generous measure!

He stood up abruptly.

'Come up on to the roof,' he said. 'It's fairly hot just now, but it's worth it.'

The roof was more like a roof garden, with shady awnings to protect them from the worst rays of the afternoon sun. Jenny caught her breath when she looked down first on the garden – a sea of colour in an oasis of drabness – and then over the roof-tops to the slender spires of the minarets, rising into the clear, fierce warmth of the sky, the encircling, rose-red walls of the city, and the impressiveness of the High Atlas beyond. It was certainly worth climbing to the roof to see all that, and the thought struck her that on a starry night it would be even more worthwhile to make one's way up here. In fact, it would be something very much more than worthwhile.

And in spite of the things which frightened her down there in the *medina*, if she owned a house like this, in just this position, filled as it was with beautiful things, she was not so sure that she would want one day to leave it and go back to England.

She asked suddenly, because she had to know:

'Why do you live here?'

'Why?' He smiled at her as if she was a child who had asked an amusing question. 'One reason is because it's a very useful centre when you ply the kind of trade I ply – not overlooking the gun-running!' and she knew he was laughing at her. 'Another is that I like it. I like England, too, and Italy – but here I feel I belong, somehow. It's important to belong somewhere, you know.'

'Yes.' She agreed with him, soberly. She herself no longer had a home, and she had no ties of any kind. It was not an entirely satisfactory position to be in, and it brought a little ragged sigh up from the depths of her being, which escaped her without her knowing it.

Max Daintry, who had been leaning against the low parapet, smoking, turned and looked at her curiously. His eyes were inscrutable, and the set of his mouth was somehow remote, giving her the feeling that one could never properly know this man.

'Tell me,' he said, 'now that you've been here close upon a fortnight, how do you really like it?'

'I like it – in many ways – very much,' she answered.

'By which you mean that you like looking after the children?'

'Yes. They're not difficult to manage, and I'm already very fond of them.'

'But you're probably fond of most children?'

Jenny nodded her head.

'As a matter of fact, I am.'

'You know,' he remarked, 'you're going to make some fortunate man an extremely nice little wife some day! You have all the right ideas – I suspected that from the beginning! – and with your background and upbringing you'll cling to them through thick and thin! And that goes for the man, too – cleaving only unto him until death you do part! You and Raoul de St. Alais would have made a good pair. His ideas are very similar to yours.'

She said, stiffly,

'I like the Comte very much.'

'So you've said before.' He tossed away his only partly smoked cigarette as if he suddenly disliked the taste of it. 'You've never said you like the Comtesse.'

'I like her, too – in a – in a lesser way!'

'That's honest,' he said, resting both elbows on the parapet and staring at the roof-tops opposite. 'Don't you want to know how I managed to persuade her to let me take you out today? And even so, she had no idea I intended to bring you here for lunch!'

'Oh!' Jenny exclaimed, and felt her face suddenly flaming under the deep shade of the awning. He was looking round at her again, and his eyes were now definitely mocking her, and her own eyes grew confused. 'She was perfectly nice about it—'

'Of course!' The heavy mockery in his voice made her wonder whether it was his wish to increase her embarrassment. 'But then, I have my own methods of subduing the unsubduable! – of dealing with the intractable! It's never terribly difficult, when you bring a battery of personal charm to bear upon the opposition. But naturally you guessed all that?'

Jenny's colour spread wildly for a moment, and then faded all at once. There was something harsh in his voice – something which told her that this was his method of paying her back for the bad opinion she had formed of him at the beginning of their acquaintance. But the harshness was a little unfair, she thought, especially after his kindness in showing her so much during the morning. She swallowed noticeably, wishing earnestly that she had declined to permit him to act as her host, and all at once he straightened himself at the roof edge and turned upon her so quickly that she actually backed a step.

'You little idiot!' he said – but the mockery was gone from his tone, and it was only harsh. Looking up timidly into his face she saw that it was dark and harsh, too. 'You're free to go wherever you want to go while you remain here in Marrakesh, and *I'm* free to ask anyone here to my house I wish to ask. Do you understand what I mean by that? – I'm perfectly free to behave as I please!'

'Y-yes,' she answered, and as if fascinated by the condemning anger in his grey eyes she stared into them. She stared until all at once something happened to her that had never happened to her before, and she felt breathless – just as if she had run thoughtlessly up a steep flight of stairs and been forced to halt at the top because of an odd sensation in the region of her heart. She even wanted to put a hand up over her heart to stop it behaving so eccentrically, while the blood seemed to be pounding heavily through her veins. 'Y-yes,' she stammered again.

'Good!' he exclaimed, but his black brows remained almost fiercely knitted together, and there was no softening of the expression on his face. He stood so close to her that there could not have been more than a foot of space between them, and as she looked up at him with her head slightly thrown back she noticed yet again what a strong jaw he had, and what an uncompromisingly strong face his was, and the thought sped swiftly, regretfully through her mind:

'If only he and I had started off by being friends! . . .

He *would* make a good friend! ...' And something hurt dully inside her because she had the feeling that he despised her, and in any case he probably picked his friends with care. The impecunious governess employed by a long-standing acquaintance – if, indeed, she was nothing more! – was scarcely likely to be numbered amongst them!

And then all at once he disarmed her completely by relaxing and smiling at her in a whimsical fashion at the same time.

'You have a bad effect on me,' he told her. 'You always make me want to fight – and we're neither of us Irish!' And then he lightly caught her by the arm and led her towards the flight of steps leading down from the roof. 'Come back into the cool and have some tea,' he said.

The rest of the afternoon passed pleasantly enough, and while they drank mint tea made in a silver tea-pot by the servant who carried in the tray, and served in small glasses with a great deal of sugar so that it tasted more like a liqueur – although a very refreshing liqueur, Jenny had to admit – Max Daintry talked to her in the manner of a perfectly correct but friendly host, and showed her part of his collection of ancient coins, as well as a magnificent collection of Egyptian scarabs which he owned. He confessed to a weakness for Egypt, where he had once lived for a time, and she gathered that the whole northern part of Africa fascinated him. The sharp colour contrasts, the fierce sunshine, were things he would be loath to give up in order to go home and live in England, where he owned property passed on to him by his father. Although he admitted at the same time that he liked England.

'And you are very English,' he said deliberately, looking at her strangely.

Jenny looked away quickly.

'It seems a pity,' she remarked, 'that owning a house in England you should never visit it. What sort of a house is it? Is it large or small?'

'Reasonably large – in fact, quite large. But not too large to be live-in-able.'

'Where?' she asked.

'In Hampshire, not far from the sea. An old house. I'm sure you would find it attractive,' he added with a curious smile.

'I have always thought,' Jenny agreed, with a tiny glow in her eyes, 'that to own a house of that sort would give one more pleasure than almost anything else, particularly if it has a big garden. And Hampshire is a lovely county. My home is in Dorset – or at least,' she corrected herself, with a sudden, sharp sigh, 'it was!'

'Dorset and Hampshire,' Daintry remarked, studying her reflectively – 'not so very far apart! Perhaps one of these days you'll go back to Dorset – and you may even visit Hampshire?'

And then he put away the scarabs and the coins, and stood up and announced that if they were not to antagonize Célestine unreasonably Jenny had better be returned to her charges. Jenny, who had enjoyed the last hour more than any other part of the day, felt as if she had been brought brutally back to reality, and she stood up quickly, repressing a sigh which he might misunderstand if she allowed it to escape her.

When they arrived back at the St. Alais house the Comtesse appeared at once and greeted Daintry with a radiant smile. She was wearing a cocktail dress of highly sophisticated black, and there were diamonds in her ears and sparkling at her throat and wrists. By contrast with the sable quality of her dress her hair flamed brilliantly in the sombre magnificence of the St. Alais main entrance hall, and her skin was positively breathtaking. Looking at her, Jenny was sure she had never seen anyone even a tithe as lovely before, and she was sure that her impact on anyone belonging to the male sex must be devastating.

'So you're back!' she said, but she spared not so much as a side-glance for Jenny. 'This young woman' – merely indicating the governess with her hand – 'is in great demand these days! Si Mohammed Menebhi is taking her out to lunch tomorrow, and you've entertained her all day. What a thing it is to be young and unattached!' But her confident eyes, fixed on the man's face, conveyed no yearning to be in Jenny's shoes herself – she was obviously more than satisfied with her own status, and eminently sure of herself in every way.

Max Daintry looked sideways at Jenny.

'You didn't tell me,' he said quietly, 'about your lunch appointment tomorrow.' She thought that his lips curled. 'I had no idea governesses were so gay!'

Jenny was unable to think of anything to say, and the Comtesse answered for her:

'My dear Max, don't make the girl uncomfortable! – She can't help being attractive, can she? And there is no reason at all why a pretty governess shouldn't be gay

– certainly not when she happens to be my employee. I'm all for it!'

Her smile looked as if it had been delicately painted on her lips, and there was a hint of derisive amusement in her eyes as she gazed up at Max. He gazed back at her for a few moments with a kind of cynical appreciation, and then he turned to the door and ignored Jenny.

'Women are beyond me,' he remarked, in a cool clipped tone. 'I never pretend to understand them.'

'Darling, that's all part of our attraction,' Célestine murmured, slipping a hand inside his arm and moving with him out into the patio. And just before she started to move towards the stairs Jenny heard the Comtesse add, 'You won't be late tonight, will you, Max? Last time you kept me waiting a full five minutes . . .'

And Jenny fled hastily in the direction of her own quarters.

CHAPTER NINE

JENNY was not sorry, from purely selfish motives, when the next day she was unable to keep her luncheon appointment with Si Mohammed Menebhi because her small charge Louis developed feverish symptoms. The Comtesse looked vexed and disapproving when she saw how he clung to the English governess's hand, and declared that she thought it would be perfectly all right for Jenny to leave him in the charge of Nerida, and that in any case Dr. Le Croix would be summoned, and he was used to Louis's sudden little up-flarings of temperature.

'Do you mean,' Jenny said, looking at her in amazement, 'that although it is my job to look after the children you would prefer it if I kept this luncheon date and left someone else to do the thing I am paid to do? Surely Dr. Le Croix would think that very odd!'

Célestine shrugged her shoulders impatiently.

'If I approve of your leaving Louis I can hardly see that it matters what anyone else thinks,' she answered sharply. 'And Si Mohammed is an old friend, and I promised him that you would lunch with him today. I don't think it fair to put him off.'

'But I couldn't dream of leaving Louis,' Jenny said, with so much quiet determination in her tone that her employer looked at her in surprise, and then elevated her eyebrows.

'Yesterday you did what you wished to do to please

93

yourself and no one else,' she pointed out. 'Today I think you should do what I wish you to do.'

Jenny stood up, her deep blue eyes reflecting faint distress and astonishment.

'But surely—?' she began.

'It is important to me that you keep your appointment today,' Célestine told her coldly.

'And I would much rather that you didn't insist!'

'Oh,' the Comtesse exclaimed, with an almost infuriated look of dislike, 'you and Raoul are so much alike – it is duty, duty, duty with you both, all the time! I have no patience with such self-appointed martyrs!'

And then, very much to Jenny's relief, but also rather to her surprise – because she had been afraid that the Comtesse had been going to insist that she went out and made a pretence of enjoying herself instead of performing the job she was paid for at a time when the job should be the all-important thing – she flounced out of the room and slammed the door sharply behind her, although the disturbance and the unnecessary noise she created caused her small son, who had been dropping off into an uneasy doze, to open his eyes and wail pathetically.

Jenny managed to soothe him, and at last, while she sat beside him, he did drop off into an uneasy slumber, although his temperature was still high, and when the bustling little French doctor arrived to examine him he was once more somewhat jarringly prodded into wakefulness.

But Dr. Le Croix saw nothing in his condition to cause the least alarm.

'It is nothing serious,' he said. 'Merely the climate.

94

The child should be sent home to France.'

'You mean that he is subject to this sort of thing?' Jenny asked.

'Oh, yes – nothing extraordinary in a child of his years and delicate constitution.' His very bright dark eyes surveyed the slim figure of the governess with open appreciation. 'You are new here?' he asked. 'I haven't seen you before.'

'No, I am quite new,' Jenny admitted.

The French doctor picked up his black bag and beamed at her approvingly.

'In that case, I hope you will stay,' he said. 'Good for the children – good for us all to have an attractive fresh face in our midst!' In spite of his flattering look and speech Jenny judged him to be the type to have a comfortable wife and probably several near-grown-up children of his own, but she smiled at him pleasantly. 'Good day to you, mademoiselle,' he concluded, and sketched her a portly bow.

She did not see anything more of the Comtesse that day, and as her lunch was brought to her in the nursery she saw nothing of the Comte until about three o'clock in the afternoon, when she went out into the central courtyard for a breath of fresh air and an opportunity to stretch her legs in one of the cool colonnades.

The Comte was already there, walking up and down between the slender marble columns, and she thought that there was a decidedly harassed expression on his face as he paced beside the long rectangular pool with the waterlilies floating on it.

At sight of her he came hastening up, and as always he greeted her with excessive politeness, his eyes lighting as if with pleasure.

'Ah, Miss Armitage!' he exclaimed, and placed one of the long wicker chairs for her. 'It was good of you to forgo your own pleasure in order to remain with my son! It was extremely good of you.'

'But I had no wish to do anything else,' Jenny assured him, looking up at him from the depths of her comfortable chair and thinking that he and his wife were unusual employers in that they both, for some reason, made a point of her having a taste of social life while she was with them. 'I was quite happy to remain with Louis, and in any case it is my job.'

'And you weren't very much disappointed because your appointment to lunch had to be postponed?'

'Of *course* not.'

She thought that his expression not only lightened, but he appeared surprised – and, she was secretly certain, relieved.

'I understood from my wife that you – that it would be something of a disappointment.'

Jenny shook her head, and she smiled at him in a way she reserved for people who for some reason appealed to her as not being entirely happy, and in need of some sort of solace and consolation being brought to them.

'Nothing of the kind,' she said. 'As a matter of fact—' And then she broke off, thinking that she had better not contradict too flatly anything that the Comtesse had said.

The Comte brought a chair close to her side, and when he was seated in it he looked at her gravely, earnestly.

'Miss Armitage,' he said quietly, 'I would like you to know that, while you are with us, anything you do not wish to do, at any time, you most certainly must not allow yourself to be forced into doing! You are your own mistress, free to express your dislikes, as well as any inclinations of your own. I would not like to feel that you were – coerced . . .'

He had offered her a cigarette, and as he held his lighter to the tip of it he leaned rather near to her and looked long and carefully into her eyes. She realized at once what he was trying to tell her – that so far as Si Mohammed was concerned, or any other man his wife might decide would be a suitable escort for her, she was at liberty to please herself entirely, and that she must not allow Célestine to impose her own will on her. Which, if she had weakly given way over the lunch appointment today, would most certainly have been the case!

She tried to assure him, in as tactful a manner as she could, that there was no danger of anything of that sort happening, and then because she thought it wise she changed the conversation by introducing instead the subject of Louis and his tendency to run high temperatures. Instantly the father's face grew much more openly anxious. He tossed away the end of his own cigarette, and ground it beneath his heel on the black and white tessellated pavement.

'I wish I knew – I wish I knew what is the best thing to do with Louis,' he exclaimed, as if the words were wrung out of him. 'And, if it comes to that, little Simone, too, although somehow I do not feel she will ever present as great a problem as Louis. She is very much her mother's daughter, whereas Louis—' He broke off. 'Sometimes I wish that my mother—'

'Your mother is English,' Jenny said gently. 'You would like Louis to go to England?'

He lifted his troubled dark eyes and gazed at her.

'I don't know – but sometimes I think it would be a good plan.'

'And your mother, Lady Berringer, would, of course, be in a position to keep an eye on him, even if he went to boarding school?'

'Yes.'

She stared at the pool, reflecting like a mirror the deep blue of the afternoon sky. From the garden the scent of oranges reached them, mixed with the even more disturbing perfume of the lilies that rioted beneath the hot sun.

'And – your wife?' she asked hesitantly.

'My wife would like Louis to be sent to school in France. But there we would neither of us be near him, and my mother would have no influence over him – and he is very young yet!'

Jenny recognized the problem, and she felt herself sighing inwardly for him.

'I suppose,' she said, more slowly, 'that there is no possibility that you will ever return to live in France? I noticed a beautiful little picture of a lovely old French château, set amongst vineyards, in the library. Is that – does that belong to you?'

'Yes,' he admitted, and his voice all at once was openly bitter. 'It is mine, but Célestine has quite made up her mind that she does not ever wish to return to live in France – a few weeks in Paris during a part of each

year is the most she desires to see of her own country! –
and Marrakesh for her holds so much charm that it is
highly unlikely we shall ever return to France – to
live.'

And she knew by the faint weariness, and the wist-
fulness, of his tone, that to return to France, and his
lovely old château, and not to be forced to leave it
again for the strange exotic brilliance of life in a North
African desert town was one of his secret dreams.

And looking at him, and his sad, disillusioned face,
she asked herself why he had married Célestine, and
imagined that in her was a suitable life partner for a
man who still possessed ideals. And the only answer she
could think of was that it was her beauty that had
enthralled him – as it had probably enthralled a good
many other men!

Including – Max Daintry . . .?

They talked for a while longer on matters less likely to
perturb either of them, and then Jenny decided that
she must return to her charge, although she knew by
the Comte's look that he was reluctant to let her go.
She realized that in her he sensed a sympathizer in his
problems, and since she was truly feminine her sympathy, once aroused, was liable to escape her without
the volition of her own will, and the Comte de St. Alais
was badly in need of feminine sympathy just then.

Jenny would not admit to herself that he could possibly see anything else in her that would account for the
obvious pleasure he felt when she devoted a little of her
time to him.

The following day Louis improved, but his improvement was so slow that Jenny spent practically all her time near to him. She read to him and told him stories, while Nerida looked after Simone, and kept her away from any possible infection, and by the end of the third day Jenny felt that the little boy had become curiously dependent on her, and she wished she knew the best thing to advise about his future.

His grandmother came to see him on the afternoon of the third day, and Jenny's first impression of her was confirmed. She was lovely for her age, poised, charming and friendly, if not particularly practical, and although she did not look or behave very much like a grandmother Jenny knew that the little boy welcomed her visit. She brought him unsuitable books and *bonbons*, but she stayed talking to him and holding his hand beside his bed until as he did with Jenny, he fell into one of his more tranquil dozes, which in this case looked as if it was going to last well into the evening, and meant that he really was very much better.

If only he hadn't looked quite so much like Dresden china instead of a sturdy boy Jenny would have been happier about him.

Before Lady Berringer left she told Jenny that there was to be an important dance at one of the more modern of the French luxury hotels on the following night, and that her daughter-in-law, she knew, was planning a party for it. The party would have dinner in the hotel beforehand, and then attend the dance, and Lady Berringer herself and her companion, Esther Harringay, would be two of those who would make up the party. Others would probably be one or two friends of Célestine's and, of course, the Comte – if he could be persuaded to put in an appearance at a dance, which was not the sort of thing he enjoyed.

'And I've got an idea that Célestine intends you to come along with us as well,' Lady Berringer told Jenny, smiling at her. 'I said you'd have quite a nice social life here, didn't I? And so you will, unless I'm very much mistaken. Célestine may even make an attempt to marry you off to someone she considers suitable,' with a sudden touch of dryness to her smile. 'She's rather good at that sort of thing — and if you have no desire to be married off just yet, beware, child!'

Suddenly she touched Jenny's cheek, as if she liked the look of it.

'You're a nice child, too — and I know my son thinks so!' She sighed unexpectedly. 'Poor Raoul! . . . Sometimes I think . . .' But she did not voice her thoughts aloud, and instead she looked again at Jenny and asked rather curiously: 'Have you seen anything more of Max Daintry?'

'Yes,' Jenny admitted. 'I had lunch with him the other day, and he showed me some of the sights of Marrakesh.'

Lady Berringer elevated one skilfully darkened eyebrow.

'With or without my daughter-in-law's approval?'

Jenny thought she saw something quizzical in the other's expression — quizzical and surprised — and for no reason at all she flushed.

'With the Comtesse's permission and approval, of course.'

'H'm!' Lady Berringer exclaimed. The quizzical

look vanished from her eyes, and she studied Jenny more keenly. 'What do you think of him?' she asked. 'Do you like him?'

To her acute annoyance Jenny felt herself flushing almost uncontrollably.

'Yes – yes, of course,' she answered, although she honestly did not know whether she liked him or disliked him – or liked him very much! 'He – I think he thought I felt a bit strange here, and being partly English—'

'But only partly, my dear!' Lady Berringer reminded her. 'The other half of him is unpredictable Italian, and in any case he must be nearly thirty-five – he could even be a year or two older. And he's lived every one of those years to the full! Remember that, my dear child, if you ever begin to feel that he has a rather powerful attraction – and personally I feel he could be extremely attractive if one saw enough of him, and if for some reason or other he *wanted* one to be impressed by that essential masculinity of his!' There was a bright, inscrutable smile in her blue eyes as they rested on the girl in front of her, and she picked up her immaculate white handbag and gloves and moved towards the nursery door. 'It's the one thing about him you can't ignore, isn't it? – that positive, iron-hard, unquestionable strength of his. And it would be rather like hurling oneself against a stone wall – with as much risk of being badly battered! – if you wanted something he was not prepared to give!'

At the door she paused and looked back at Jenny, and there was no longer any hint of a smile in her eyes. In fact, for a moment, she looked almost grave.

'*Au revoir*, my dear,' she said. 'I shall probably see you at the dance tomorrow night. I wouldn't like you to be hurt – ever! You're much too young, and much too gentle!'

When the Comtesse made her appearance in the nursery just before dinner she was looking much more affable than she had done for three days, and there was a kind of amiable approval in her eyes when she looked towards Jenny, seated in the wide nursery window with a pile of small garments that required buttons and an odd darn here and there, while her son slumbered peacefully.

'I must say,' she remarked, 'your sense of duty has been very high over the past three days, and I'm quite sure I ought to be delighted because that agency in London sent you to me. And, as a matter of fact, I am' – with a brittle smile at Jenny – 'and I also feel that you've earned something in the nature of a small reward.'

Jenny looked up at her a trifle anxiously, waiting for what was coming next. But all that did come was confirmation of the hint Lady Berringer had dropped her during the afternoon.

'How would you like to go to a dance?' Célestine asked. 'Tomorrow night?'

Jenny glanced for a moment at Louis, but his mother said impatiently:

'Oh, Louis is sufficiently recovered to be safely left with Nerida for one evening, at least, and all work and no play makes Jill a dull girl! The dance is at the Splendide – one of the newer hotels – and I am getting up a party for it, so I think you will find it rather fun.

Being young you naturally adore dancing?'

'I haven't done a great deal of it,' Jenny confessed – and she might have added that she had had very little opportunity up to date to indulge any secret passion she might have for the type of ballroom dancing her employer had in mind.

Célestine surveyed her with raised eyebrows, and a cool, amused smile on her lips.

'Nevertheless, I'm sure you do dance beautifully, and while you are with me I want you to have as good a time as possible,' she said magnanimously. 'Although I pay you a salary, I have no desire at all to treat you as if you were nothing more than an employee, and there wouldn't be much point in your having come all the way from England to a place like Marrakesh if you couldn't enjoy yourself occasionally.' She sank down gracefully in an armchair and lighted herself a cigarette, although Jenny would have preferred the air of her small charge's bedroom kept free from the taint of cigarette-smoke. 'Have you got anything suitable to wear? – apart from that white dress you wore when we went to the Benoîts?'

'I have a pale primrose one,' Jenny replied. 'It's quite new, and it's my only other evening dress.'

Célestine looked at her consideringly.

'Pale primrose?' she echoed. And then she finally nodded her head in approval. 'With your hair, and those eyes, that should make you look rather like a primrose yourself. And I will lend you my cape again, and you can borrow anything else of mine you are short of – gloves, an evening bag, anything of that sort.' Jenny was a little slow in thanking her, for she could not altogether understand the reason why someone who employed her as a governess should be anxious about her appearance at a dance, and be willing to pass on to her things of her own in order to improve that appearance, or at least make the best of it, and she could only conclude that the Comtesse was naturally rather generous – or perhaps, having been a model herself at one time in her career, she liked to see other young women looking attractive.

Célestine stood up and smiled carelessly at Jenny.

'There is a very smart boutique in the French town,' she said, 'where you can buy anything you want or are in need of. And if you'd like an advance of salary for the purpose I can always let you have it.'

And then she went out, leaving Jenny wondering still more why, apparently, it was essential for the English girl to look always at her best. And she could not arrive at a satisfactory answer.

CHAPTER TEN

THE Splendide was not as huge as the Mamounia, but it had a beautiful ballroom, and on the night of the dance that ballroom was almost uncomfortably crowded.

Jenny had never seen anything quite like it before, and after having had dinner in the magnificent dining-room at a table that was brilliant with flowers and the cynosure of a good many pairs of eyes because such a large, distinguished, and obviously gay party sat down at it, she was feeling overawed and as if nothing had the sharp edge of reality. At dinner she had sat between Si Mohammed – a Si Mohammed who was cool, because she had broken a date with him, although his eyes could not resist the temptation to admire her openly – and Esther Harringay, Lady Berringer's companion, who looked quite attractive in a dress of orchid-mauve chiffon. She was one of those people to whom evening dress lent an undeniable distinction, and at the same time she appeared younger, and her grey eyes were so unusually beautiful that Jenny was quite fascinated by them. The Comte, who was at the head of the table, had known her, apparently, since they were both scarcely out of their teens, and Jenny did not miss the fact that whenever he addressed his mother's companion there was a gentleness in his tone, and a smile in his eyes, that brought an unmistakable and very revealing light blush to her cheeks.

Jenny thought, with quick sympathy, that Esther gave herself away entirely every time that blush appeared, and she wondered whether the Comte had the least idea of the kind of effect he had on the still flower-like spinster. The Comtesse, who was looking her most vividly beautiful in dark emerald green, with emeralds sending out shafts of dazzling green fire at her perfect throat, ears and wrists, made a point, it seemed, of ignoring Miss Harringay unless bare politeness forced her to address a remark to her, and then Jenny was sure that the contempt in her eyes had a withering effect on Esther, who probably sensed that it was deliberate.

Apart from Lady Berringer – who was perfect in pearl-pink silk and diamonds – there were two other young men, and another young woman, who helped to make up the party, and as champagne flowed freely it was a very cheerful party, although Jenny did no more than barely sip at her champagne, being quite unused to it and uncertain of the effect it might have on her.

She danced afterwards in the ballroom with Si Mohammed, and with both the young men whose acquaintance she had made at the dinner-table. One of them was a young French officer who paid her many fluent compliments, and the other, rather a Latin type, danced the tango with so much skill and enthusiasm that Jenny felt that on the whole she preferred the French officer, who danced badly, probably because he never stopped talking and telling her how 'adorably' English she was.

She had one dance with the Comte, who was plainly not very keen on the exercise, but handled her as if she was made of fragile china, and talked to her in his courteous fashion which never seemed to fail him, while his wife was claimed by the latin type. And then Si Mohammed, whose steps suited hers perfectly, and who was probably the best-looking man in the room, led her out into a kind of ante-room where the cool air coming in at the open windows was highly welcome after the heat and the crush of the ballroom.

Si Mohammed put her into a comfortable basket chair, asked her whether he could get her some refreshment, which she declined, and then took the chair beside her and asked her reproachfully why she had broken her luncheon date with him.

'But didn't the Comtesse tell you?' she asked, looking at him in wide-eyed surprise. 'Louis was not well, and I could not possibly leave him. It was not a question of deliberately breaking a date.'

'Are you quite sure?' he asked, leaning towards her, and confusing her by the sudden brilliance of his dark eyes, and the eagerness which lay behind the brilliance. 'Célestine said nothing of Louis's illness, but she did say you found it impossible to meet me after all. I was very much disappointed, and – a little hurt, too.'

'Oh!' Jenny exclaimed, and frowned, because it was against her natural instincts ever to appear rude to anyone. 'In that case, I am sorry, but I naturally thought the Comtesse would tell you the truth. Louis is very delicate, and it is my job to look after him, and there was no other course open to me.'

'Never mind,' he said softly, and she thought that he was leaning unnecessarily near to her, and the blaze the discreetly shaded lights made of his shining golden head was almost dazzling. 'There will be other occasions – many occasions, I hope! – and we will trust that in future the small Louis will be more considerate. Perhaps one night you will dine with me?'

'I – I don't know . . .' Jenny stammered.

'You are so lovely,' he told her, his voice sounding a trifle indistinct. 'I have never seen anyone quite like you before, and your eyes are like blue flowers.' As she hastily averted them one of his hands lightly touched hers that were loosely clasped in her lap. 'Are all Englishwomen as lovely as you, or are you just a rarity? Because if you are, I would like to be the one to admire you constantly, and to tell you how glad I am you decided to leave England behind you! If you hadn't done so – and that is a thought I prefer not to dwell on! – my life would have remained incomplete, because nothing like you would have come my way, and all my days I would have wondered what it was I was missing. Now I have seen you, and I know—'

'Please!' Jenny requested, shrinking instinctively back from him as both his hands imprisoned hers, and before she could prevent his doing so he carried her fingers up to his handsome mouth and dropped kisses as light as a butterfly's touch on each of her delicate, pale-pink nails. 'Please—' giving a determined tug in the hopes of freeing her fingers – 'Mr. Menebhi—!'

But he grasped them so tightly that it was impossible to free them, and a wave of annoyance swept over her.

'I would like to return to the others,' she said, with much more sharpness, 'and you must remember that I hardly know you—'

'Which, at least, is not my fault!' he reminded her. 'It is now nearly a week since we met, and although I have longed to see you again you have remained persistently elusive. If only you will let me know when I can see you again, without all these others about us, I will endeavour to be patient, though patience where you are concerned is not easy.'

'I am not entitled to very much free time,' she tried to put him off. 'It is not a question of just fixing a time to meet anyone, because when you are looking after children anything might happen, and — and in any case—'

'Yes?' He eased the grip on her hands, but retained them determinedly nevertheless.

Jenny looked wildly round the dim ante-room, with its Moorish arches and silken curtains flowing beneath the arches. There was a glimpse of enormous stars peering in at a tall window near by, and palms waving on a balcony outside. Dance music reached them, but it seemed very distant and muted, and apparently the ante-room was unpopular with everyone save themselves. If it were not for the fact that the Comtesse would probably be the reverse of pleased if she rebuffed him outright Jenny knew that she would have done so without hesitation, for in spite of his spectacular looks and his flattering speech there was something about this young Moor which repelled her a little, and something else about him which even alarmed her. His dark, caressing eyes seemed almost to gloat over her, and the ruthless strength of his beautifully-shaped hands struck something cold and warning to her heart. The very thought of dining with him alone — or just the two of them together in a hotel such as this, or perhaps even a smaller, more intimate restaurant – sent waves of revulsion breaking over her, and she was afraid a certain amount of her feeling must be given away by her expression.

'Please,' she repeated – 'I really do think we ought to rejoin the others.'

'And I am not in any hurry whatsoever to rejoin the others!' Something hard and amused appeared in his eyes, and he laughed softly – so softly that it was almost sinister. 'How deliciously young you are, little Jenny Armitage – and how sweet it would be to teach you to grow up! . . .'

The movement of a curtain at the far end of the room surprised him and he looked up, and Jenny looked round quickly over her shoulder just as the curtain was carelessly swept aside and Max Daintry stood negligently looking in upon them.

'Ah – Miss Armitage!' he exclaimed, and sauntered, or so it seemed to her, towards the middle of the room where they sat. 'The Comtesse told me you had joined her party, and I was wondering whether you would permit me to tread on your toes in the next dance? I really mean tread on your toes, by the way, because dancing is not one of the things I do well . . .' He was looking at Si Mohammed with a cold, almost a set expression on his face, and though his words were light the way he uttered them lent them a touch of grimness. Si Mohammed stood up and looked back at him with an equally unconcealed dislike in his expression, and for a moment Jenny felt as if there was a kind of tension in the atmosphere between them. Then Daintry added curtly, belatedly: ''Evening, Menebhi! The Comtesse was looking for you just now, and I can take Miss Armitage back to the ballroom when she feels like it.'

Jenny realized – and she had realized it almost immediately – that he was well aware that the Moor had been holding both her hands, and that there had been very little space indeed between them when he appeared under the arch. But whether he imagined she had approved of the hand-holding she had no idea.

'Miss Armitage and I were sitting this dance out,' Si Mohammed answered softly, in his perfect French. There was a tight curl to his lips, but his eyes were all at once inscrutable. 'But if the Comtesse is looking for me—'

'She is.'

'Then I had better go.'

He bowed – stiffly, formally – to Jenny, and then moved in a lithe and sinuous fashion across the floor of the ante-room in the direction of the arch. As the curtains fell to behind him Jenny found her heart thudding violently and she looked upwards almost apprehensively at Max Daintry.

'Well?' he asked. 'Are you ready?'

'To – to dance?' she asked.

'No. To return to Lady Berringer. She's probably better able to keep an eye on you than anyone else, and it's quite obvious that an eye – for the rest of this evening, at any rate – ought to be kept on you!'

There was so much coolness and contempt in his tone that she knew at once that his opinion of her was low – lower than at any time since he had known her.

Even his look swept over her disparagingly, although in the dress of primrose cotton, with a row of seed pearls about her slender neck, and her burnished hair like a crown about her shapely small head, she looked particularly young and vulnerable – and perhaps also a little afraid of she was not quite sure what – and the picture she made should have banished anything in the nature of harshness.

But no doubt, as she realized, Max Daintry was impervious to the slightly immature appearance of a young Englishwoman of twenty-four. He was, as Lady Berringer had phrased it, 'of positive, iron-hard, and unquestionable strength,' and to beat oneself against it would be like beating oneself against the unyielding cliffs of her native Dorset.

She only knew that as she walked at his side back to the ballroom she felt as if her age had shrunk considerably, that he was infinitely removed from her, and that in any case he was anxious to have very little to do with her, and to say nothing at all to her just then. He handed her over to Lady Berringer, and the latter looked up into his dark face with a semi-amused expression on her own, and something mildly provocative in her extremely youthful blue eyes.

'Dear me!' she exclaimed. 'Have you been rescuing a damsel in distress, or is it merely that you like interfering, Max? Si Mohammed returned here just now with a brow as black as thunder, and Célestine has taken him on to the floor to soothe his ruffled feelings. Was it you, by any chance, who ruffled them?'

She looked for a moment at Jenny, whose abashed, downcast expression said a good deal, and then into the man's sombre, cynical grey eyes, and he gave her a kind of cold smile before turning away to leave them.

'You can take it that I like interfering,' he said, and Lady Berringer looked in a more openly amused fashion at Jenny.

'Never mind, child,' she said. 'The evening is young yet, and we must find someone really nice for you to dance with.'

But it was the Comte who asked Jenny to dance the next dance, and the young Frenchman who took her in search of refreshment. Although paying her extravagant compliments, he was the type of young man who always behaved correctly, and with him, at least, she was able to relax and be at ease, even if she did not enjoy herself. And it was impossible to enjoy herself when she saw Daintry having dance after dance with Célestine, whose expression gave away the fact that in his arms she was almost blissfully happy, and Jenny felt sick with shame for her, pitifully sorry for the Comte, and miserably unhappy about herself because something had happened to her, she now knew with aching certainty, which could never be put right, and under these conditions this evening when she was meant to enjoy herself – in the words of Célestine – was turning into something like a nightmare. In any case, she wished it would end soon.

She was amazed when she stopped dancing with the French officer to find Max suddenly at her elbow, and she was still more amazed when he said coolly,

'Well, do you want to try dancing with me, or would you prefer to come outside for a breath of air?'

Words failed her for a moment, and he took her arm and led her back through the fatal ante-room and out on to the balcony where the palms in brass tubs waved gently in the night air. Larger palms in the courtyard below them towered past the balcony and seemed to be reaching for the stars, and the same night air made a kind of dry music of their rustling leaves.

'I don't think it's cold enough tonight for you to need a wrap,' he said, 'and in any case I don't propose to remain out here long. But I want to tell you one thing – if you persist in playing with fire you're bound to get burnt, do you know that?'

She felt herself freeze into immobility, and she looked at him stiffly.

'What do you mean?' she asked, in a voice that was just as stiff.

He shrugged slightly.

'Simply this, Jenny Wren – that unless you wish to become involved in something you won't like you will refrain from accepting invitations to lunch and so forth with a young man like Si Mohammed Menebhi. I should have thought that having lunch with him would have taught you enough, but tonight, apparently, you were still prepared to keep him on a loose rein. Or perhaps it wasn't such a loose rein?'

Jenny felt her face go pale, at first with astonishment, and then with indignation, and as she answered him her voice quivered.

'As I haven't yet had lunch with Si Mohammed I don't know what you're talking about, and tonight – tonight I was not encouraging him, as I am well aware you imagined I was. And in any case – what is wrong

115

with Si Mohammed?'

'He's a Moor, for one thing – oh, you wouldn't think it to look at him, I know, but he is a pure bred Moor, and very proud of his ancestry if it comes to that – and you're English, and however much those good looks of his might appeal to your impressionable English heart you will do well to resist the temptation to fall for them. Unless, of course, you don't object to sharing a husband with several other wives?' with considerable dryness. 'And wouldn't even object to being shut up yourself in the modern equivalent of a harem?'

In the white light of the moon, riding serenely high in the purple night sky, Jenny turned even paler, and she swallowed hard.

'I think,' she said, in a faint voice, 'you are very unpleasant.'

'Thank you,' Daintry returned, and accorded her a little bow.

She looked at him witheringly for a moment, and then turned to make her way off the balcony, but he caught her by the arm. His hard fingers bruised her bare flesh – for the second time that night masculine fingers had gripped her roughly.

'What do you mean,' he asked, with the same harsh note in his voice, 'by saying that you haven't lunched with Menebhi? You were going to lunch with him the day after I showed you a few of the sights of Marrakesh.'

Jenny succeeded in wrenching her arm free.

'I was,' she said, 'because it was the Comtesse's wish. But neverthless I didn't. Louis had a temperature and I couldn't leave him. Tonight is the first time I have been out since I saw you last.'

'Is that true?' he asked, looking at her keenly.

'No,' she answered, laughing rather recklessly, 'it's a lie I've cooked up to deceive you. And now do you mind if we go inside?'

But once again his fingers encircled her arm, and this time they really did hurt her.

'Is that the truth?' he demanded.

'I've just told you, I'm not above distorting the truth if it suits me.' She winced beneath the bruising pressure of his fingers. 'You're hurting me,' she told him, more faintly. 'And it's cold out here. I really would like to go in.'

'I'm sorry, Jenny,' he said quickly, quietly, releasing her, and she was so astonished because he actually sounded sorry that the fact that he had twice called her Jenny in a matter of minutes passed her by. 'I should have known that a vicar's daughter wouldn't stoop so low as to, as you've just said, distort the truth,' with a shade more dryness. 'But Célestine gave me plainly to understand that you did accept that invitation, and she said nothing about Louis's temperature.'

'Then you ought to believe Célestine instead of me,' Jenny half whispered. 'After all, I'm only someone she employs, and you've known her a very long while, haven't you?'

CHAPTER ELEVEN

FOR the next week Jenny was allowed to carry out her normal duties as a governess in the St. Alais household and occupy herself in her spare time in any way she pleased, and she received no invitations from anyone which she would have preferred to decline.

She exercised the children in the garden, they were carried out each afternoon for a conventional outing in one of the big cars, and if there were visitors to the house she did not see them.

About the middle of the week the Comte announced at lunch time that it was necessary for him to fly to Paris. Jenny was a little dismayed by the news because she knew that she was going to miss his pleasant, courteous conversation at meal times, and an occasional quiet talk with him in the evenings, although Célestine apparently was left quite unshaken by the information. She did not even bother to ask him how soon he would be back, or why precisely he was going – although, as Jenny realized, she probably knew it was in connection with business – and her attitude of complete indifference struck something like a cold chill to the heart of the English girl.

To her it was a dreadful thing that a marriage, which should surely have been happy, was such an empty, comfortless thing. And when she remembered Célestine's rapt expression while she was dancing in the arms of Max Daintry she felt colder still.

The Comte left before dinner that evening, and the Comtesse dined out. Jenny had her dinner brought to her on a tray in the nursery, and she was glad of the society of the children because the house seemed strangely quiet and deserted.

For the next two days practically all her meals were brought to her in the nursery, and she saw little or nothing of the Comtesse. She took the children to a French dressmaker who was responsible for a good many of their clothes, and she took Louis to a dentist for the removal of one of his small teeth because he had been kept awake by toothache, and on the way home in the big grey car she caught a glimpse of Si Mohammed on his theatrical-looking white horse, but he was disappearing in a cloud of dust under an archway, and he did not see her.

The next day Max Daintry came to lunch, and Jenny was asked to bring the children downstairs for the meal. Max was good with the children, and they appeared to like him very much, twining their arms about him and calling him Uncle Max, while Célestine looked on with a strange, carven smile on her lovely, cool red lips.

Jenny was glad that she had to occupy herself cutting up Simone's food, supervising Louis occasionally and making certain there were no disasters at the table, such as a vase of flowers overturned, or a glass of orange squash sent cascading across the polished surface, to the danger of the lace table mats, and that she had little opportunity to be anything but aloof to Max Daintry without it seeming at all noticeable. For at least half a dozen times a day she kept recalling that picture of him dancing with the Comtesse, she remembered what Lady Berringer had said about the dangers of seeking to make an impression on him, and she had only to close her eyes to feel again the ruthless pressure of his fingers on her arm, and the steel in his voice when he warned her of encouraging Si Mohammed Menebhi.

Lady Berringer was right; he was hard. And he was hard right through! The mockery in his eyes made them dangerously attractive, and it would be impossible to doubt that Célestine – though in every other way she too was hard as unbending metal – was in love with him.

And unless he wanted to encourage her he would not meet her as often as he did. Jenny, who knew only too well how much danger she was in herself – of being battered against a stone wall? – was constantly hearing those murmured words of Célestine's when she let him out of the house after he had devoted a whole day to her, Jenny:

'*You won't be late tonight, will you, Max? Last time you kept me waiting a full five minutes.*'

There was only one interpretation to put on requests of that sort.

Jenny was thankful that she was able to refuse coffee after the meal was over because the children had to be returned to the nursery and settled down for their afternoon naps, but as she sat with some needlework on her lap she had to keep giving her head a little shake in order to shut out the picture of the man who claimed to be a fellow countryman of hers, and who knew her native Dorset, sitting in the lovely main *salon* with the

Comtesse while the two of them lingered over their coffee.

Or perhaps they would choose the even greater seclusion of the library, where possibly he would seize the opportunity to kiss Célestine's bright hair, and no one would dare to go near and interrupt them.

Jenny sewed away industriously, and she was telling herself that at least she need not meet him again that day, because tea could be served to her in the nursery, when a knock came on the nursery door, and before she could call out a 'Come in' or 'Who is it?' the door opened and the man who had not been out of her thoughts for half a minute since she left the dining-room stood looking somewhat quizzically down upon her.

'I wanted to see the children to say good-bye,' he said. 'That is, if they've had long enough for their naps? And I remembered that I hadn't said good-bye to you, either.'

Jenny stood up with assumed coolness and lifted her eyebrows.

'Of course you can say good-bye to the children,' she answered primly. 'But it wasn't exactly necessary to say good-bye to me, was it?'

His quizzical look became more noticeable.

'Well, under strictly normal circumstances, perhaps not – but I'm joining the Comte in Paris tomorrow, and I'm not quite sure how long I'll be away, so I thought it would be a good plan to lay a few injunctions upon you before I left!'

As she exclaimed 'Oh!' in a flat little voice, as if the ground had been suddenly knocked from under her feet, his smile grew more definitely amused.

'Perhaps not so much injunctions, as offer you a few suggestions,' he continued affably. 'For instance, if by any chance you should feel the need of someone who speaks your own language to exchange a few words with, Lady Berringer is delightfully understanding, and she'll be at the Mamounia for at least another fortnight. You can always get in touch with her if you want to – either her or Esther Harringay, her companion. Esther, by the way, has taken quite a fancy to you.'

'Oh!' Jenny exclaimed again, and stared down at the silk smock she had been hemming, which was still in her hand.

'I'm sorry if I said something to you the other night which annoyed you,' Daintry remarked, and she knew he was referring to Si Mohammed, and the conclusions he had arrived at. 'But you're very young, you know' – with a much fainter smile – 'and you haven't been in Marrakesh very long. All the same, I'm glad you didn't take my advice and go home.'

Jenny was silent. She was wondering why it had come as such a shock to her that he, too, was going away, and why she felt so much more than dismayed because he was going. She ought to be relieved – relieved that she wouldn't have to see anything of him, and that Célestine wouldn't be able to see him, either. and her sympathies where Raoul de St. Alais was concerned would not becalled upon to work overtime because his wife was being so blatantly unfaithful to him.

The children came running from the night nursery and threw themselves upon their visitor, and after he had picked each of them up and made a fuss of them for a short while he set them down again and held out his hand to Jenny.

'I consider it was most unfortunate the way we met,' he remarked, 'but if you hadn't such a busy little brain which you permit far too much rope, and if you weren't so eager to absorb the wrong sort of impressions, at least it would be possible for us to be friends.' The quizzical look had returned to his eyes, but his voice was more gentle than she had ever heard it before, and the close grasp of his hand was warm and somehow sustaining. 'Don't do anything of which I wouldn't approve while I'm away, little Jenny – or do you object to my calling you Jenny? Perhaps you're annoyed because I called you Jenny several times on the night of the dance?'

'Of course not,' Jenny answered, and all at once, although she felt sure he was laughing at her, she only wanted to cling to his hand, and she wished that Lady Berringer, delightful though he was, had never made those remarks about him. There was nothing unkind about him today, and despite his swarthiness the English half of him seemed very much in the ascendant. He had an English wholesomeness, an impeccability, an unquestionable masculinity. Whatever he was, and however he behaved, there was nothing weak about him – and that white-toothed smile of his had undeniable charm. Jenny felt it catch at her heart-strings, and her heart even tip-tilted dizzily while she allowed him to retain possession of her fingers.

She wished more earnestly than she had ever wished for anything in her life that they could be the friends he suggested.

'Then that's all right,' he said. 'I can go on thinking about you as Jenny, anyway.'

He looked at the sewing in her hand, at the pile of mending on the table beside her chair, and then around him at the pleasant room where she spent so much of her time, and he added the observation:

'You fit in here very well. Now that I've seen you in here, and I've also seen you with the children, watching over them at lunch time, and so forth, I realize that Célestine was lucky to get you. And whenever I want to do so I can call up a picture of you in this room!'

He gave her fingers a hard, suddenly rather brutal little squeeze, and then he let them go. His grey eyes flickered over her, from the crown of her head to the tip of her white-shod feet, and then back again to the burnished curls that framed her white brow, and she had the impression that the look was deliberate, and that he had no objection at all to her realizing that it was deliberate.

'*Au revoir*,' he said, and swung back to the door. 'Don't forget that you can always call on Lady Berringer, for advice or anything else.'

And then he was gone, and if the house had seemed empty to Jenny after the Comte had left, with the departure of Max Daintry the large, cheerful day nursery seemed suddenly bereft.

CHAPTER TWELVE

JENNY slept badly that night. In fact, for a long time she found it impossible to get to sleep at all. The moon-lit night outside her windows was disturbed by the monotonous noises of a wedding party that was making a tour of the *medina,* and the thought of the barbaric custom that permitted a girl to become the bride of a man she had never seen – and who, for that matter, had never seen her – caused her a chill of revulsion. The thin, wavering noises of the reed pipes that ac-companied the procession seemed to linger in the air even after it had passed, and to Jenny they were almost sinister sounds. She looked at the violently purple sky outside, at the white bar of moonlight on the floor of her room, and she thought that Africa – the whole of Africa – was a land of severe contrasts, and because of those contrasts it was more than a little frightening.

There was a thin veneer of civilization on the top, but underneath there was so much that was primitive, and worse than primitive. What she had seen of Mar-rakesh had taught her that. She recalled her tour of the *medina* with Max Daintry, and remembered how shocked she had been by the many evidences of squalor and grime and poverty that not even the hot sun could do much about, her shrinking from the frenzies of the medicine men and the holy men in the Djemaâ el Fna, and the monotonous rhythm of the tom-toms that beat like a discordant nerve in the ears of the unaccustomed. The beggars and the snake-charmers and the diseased animals that fled through the cobbled lanes and dark alleyways of the *medina* – these things had made her glad that Daintry was at her elbow.

And then, as she tossed restlessly in bed, she asked herself whether he had already left Marrakesh. If he had, it was unlikely that she would have him at her elbow for perhaps some while to come, and with his departure Marrakesh seemed even more sinister. She was not even sure that she had any liking for it at all.

And then she thought of Célestine, lying wakeful, perhaps, in her own extremely luxurious room, and thinking of Max Daintry just as Jenny herself was thinking of him. Missing him already – regretting his departure just as Jenny was regretting it!

For – and she buried her face suddenly in the pillow, as if she was acutely ashamed of the knowledge – they were both in love with him, and Jenny's love was so new, and so doomed to be hopeless, that it was a torment without any of the compensating pleasures love was suposed to bring in its train. But if she chose to fall in love with a man about whom even Lady Berringer had warned her – and there had been no malice in Lady Berringer's warning, she felt sure, because she admitted that in a way she liked him, and he obviously thought highly of her – and whom she herself mistrusted so much, and most of her instincts disapproved of, what could she expect but torment?

She turned over on her back, and in a panic-stricken way she stared at the moonlight, and asked herself whether it would not be the wisest thing for her to act upon the advice Daintry himself had given her, on the second occasion they met, and that was to go home to England. If she did that not only would she save herself future misery, because love once born has a habit of growing stronger, like a lusty infant, but she would be unlikely ever to see him again, and the feeling he had awakened in her might in time shrivel up. Above all she would not be forced to enter into a kind of unacknowledged competition with Célestine for the notice of a man who probably secretly despised them both, even if he found Jenny moderately entertaining, and Célestine violently attractive.

At one moment during that long and restless night Jenny was certain that the right thing would be for her to go home, but when the morning dawned, and she found that she had dozed a little after all, she was not so certain. She had her living to earn, and this was quite a good job – or, at least, it brought her a good salary, and she had become genuinely fond of her charges. Also the conditions were excellent. If she went back to England it might be a very long time before she landed herself another job where the conditions left so little to complain of.

And after the children had had their breakfast and were washed, dressed, and ready for the day, Célestine made a somewhat abrupt appearance in the nursery and announced that she was taking them all away for a few days, and that Jenny could start helping Nerida to pack.

'It's getting a bit stuffy here in Marrakesh just now,' she said, concentrating her attention on the children, who were always delighted to see her, although if she was wearing something new and special she kept them at a distance, 'and a drive into the Atlas will do us all good.' She looked up at Jenny, and surveyed her rather curiously. 'You haven't seen much of Morocco yet, so you'll enjoy this chance of a fresh glimpse of it.'

Jenny didn't like to ask her outright where they were going, and Célestine became preoccupied with deciding what the children would need to wear, and whisked open the doors of small wardrobes with the air of one who had no other immediate problems on her mind.

Jenny helped Nerida to pack, and then Nerida changed the children's nursery clothes for others that were more suited to a visit away from home, and Jenny herself put on something more formal than her candy-striped cotton. When they were ready to leave she was surprised that the Comtesse decided to leave Nerida behind, although Jenny was quite capable of coping with Louis and Simone alone, and she was even more surprised when she overheard Célestine telling the Berber servant before they left that if Lady Berringer made any attempt to contact her she was to be told that an invitation had been accepted for a few days, and that they would soon be back.

Nothing more – no information as to whom the invitation was from, or where the Comte himself might contact them if he returned unexpectedly.

But Jenny lulled a vague feeling of wonder – it was not at that stage uneasiness – by telling herself that Célestine was probably in touch with her husband by letter, and that he knew where they were going, and that the whole thing might even have been arranged before he left.

The big grey car carried them away from the closely-packed *medina*, and soon they had crossed the Djemaâ el Fna and were outside the walls of Marrakesh and heading towards the High Atlas.

Jenny looked back at the rose-pink walls of the desert town, which seemed to be glowing like blood against the light. The sunshine fell goldenly all about them, promising great heat as the day advanced, the sky was a brilliant blue, and in front beckoned the impressive grandeur of the mountains.

Because the car travelled effortlessly at speed it was not long before they reached the lower slopes of the Atlas, and then they started to climb. Red earth fell away below them, and fields of wheat and barley, olive trees and dark green pencil-like cypresses. Jenny's breath was caught by the patchwork loveliness of the scene they were leaving, while they mounted into a world that was grim and austere. Above them loomed peaks as grand as any that were to be seen in the Alps, rising against the cobalt-blue backcloth of sky in endless majesty, while the pale brown colour of the rocks was an attractive half-tone after the angry red of the desert soil.

The road twisted and turned like a corkscrew, travelling along precipitous ledges, bending in sharp, hairpin bends. The children, who were used to this kind of travel, clung to the sides of the car and laughed in sheer glee when they overhung, as it were, an appallingly steep drop, or a mountain torrent came cascading down like a silver waterfall close beside the track and disappeared into the unseen valley below them. But Jenny's heart thumped nervously from time to time, and then beat quicker with admiration.

On the seat beside the chauffeur, Célestine, in a striped silk dress and a shady hat, looked round from time to time and smiled as if the awed expression on the younger girl's face amused her.

'This is something quite new for you, Jenny,' she said — for lately she, too, had taken to calling the governess by her Christian name. 'Something rather different from England.'

There was always a faint note of contempt in her voice when she mentioned England, which made Jenny wonder whether she had ever visited it and formed a dislike of it for some reason. She might even have visited some of her husband's English relatives, and taken a dislike to them. So far as Jenny had been able to observe she had no noticeable dislike of her mother-in-law.

Hour after hour seemed to pass, and Louis and Simone sucked barley sugar and ate oranges. The impassive chauffeur at the wheel never once uttered a word, and Célestine completely ignored him.

At last, having climbed to what Jenny felt certain was practically the roof of the world, they began to descend once more, and all at once the road flattened out again, although they were by no means at the foot of the mountains. But they seemed to be hemmed in by mountains, rising like a grim encircling wall, and in the middle of an open, sandy plain Jenny saw a white, crenellated building with the road running straight towards it and an enormous entrance gate.

Jenny had an impression of a kind of fortress ringed about by loneliness cut off from the world by those endless layers of mountains, and as the car slipped through the gate and emerged in a high-walled court-yard the impression gained strength. There was another gateway facing them through which they also passed, and then she had a quick glimpse of servants standing like statues against the walls – in particular, a white-robed Negro of enormous proportions held her eyes for a moment. They alighted from the car, and then they and their baggage were being escorted through endless corridors until they finally emerged in a patio so beautiful that, in spite of her weariness, Jenny voiced her admiration for it aloud.

The sun was becoming tinged with the rosy light which meant that it was not so very far from its setting, and it gilded the oranges that hung like golden balls on the trees surrounding an exquisitely beautiful fountain. There was the cooing of doves strutting on the marble edge of the basin in which the fountain played, and marble pillars supported the balconies of the rooms which overlooked so much fairy-tale beauty. Starry white jasmine flowers surrounded the slender columns, and the air was heavy with the perfume of the jasmine and the penetrating, all-pervading scent of the oranges.

But they were not allowed to linger, and by this time the children were so tired that Jenny had to pick Simone up in her arms and carry her. Célestine walked ahead with the white-clad servant who had been in the outer courtyard to receive them, and with Louis stumbling at Jenny's heels they arrived at last in a portion of the building which, although Moorish in architecture, was modern and occidental in its furnishings.

Jenny found herself in a room of vast proportions where there was a very ornate bed covered with a silk quilt, and where there were also two smaller beds which she decided at once were for the children. Divans were ranged around the walls, piled high with cushions, and curtains of lustrous silk hung before the windows which opened outwards on to a balcony. There was a dressing-table with a silver-framed mirror on it, and silver-backed brushes and crystal flagons of perfume. And adjoining the room was an up-to-date bathroom, with embroidered face towels as well as deliciously thick bath towels draped across a chromium towel-rail.

Célestine waved a casual hand to Jenny and the children before she prepared to leave the room, and then she turned back and instructed Jenny:

'The children will be quite all right if you put them to bed straight away. Someone will bring them some supper. And then dress yourself in that pretty flowered dress of yours and join me in the next room. You'll meet our hosts downstairs.'

Jenny found herself wondering a good deal about those 'hosts' while she first bathed the children and put them to bed, and then enjoyed a bath herself and dressed according to the instructions she had received. The word 'hosts' had surprised her, but she supposed there must be a hostess as well, otherwise it would be a trifle odd.

When she rejoined the Comtesse the latter was putting the finishing touches to her evening *toilette* in a room that was very similar to the one Jenny was to share with Louis and Simone, and as always she looked extraordinarily elegant. She was adding a touch of perfume to each of her pink-lobed ears when Jenny joined her, and as she replaced the handsome crystal flagon on the dressing-table she indicated it with a flick of a scarlet-tipped finger.

'You needn't be afraid to use any of these little extras that are provided,' she said. 'They are not rubbish from the *suqs*. They started life in Paris, and would cost the earth if you tried to buy them.'

Then she looked at Jenny critically.

'Yes,' she said slowly, 'you will do very nicely.'

Jenny felt herself flushing, because there was something about Célestine's inspection which suggested it was not an idle one. And it lasted so long that her flush had time to burn like a carnation in her clear cheeks. The Comtesse laughed in her brittle fashion as she fastened a pearl stud into the ear she had just touched lightly with the stopper of the perfume bottle.

'One thing I like about you, Jenny, my dear,' she told her, 'is that although you're pretty, and you pay for dressing, you're entirely modest about it. I don't believe you know quite how pretty you are!'

Jenny, of course, made no response to this, and Célestine gave her a half amused, half contemptuous look as she led the way to the door.

'Now,' she said, 'I've got something in the nature of a surprise for you!'

CHAPTER THIRTEEN

DOWNSTAIRS in the modern part of the building Jenny and Célestine found themselves in rooms furnished entirely in western fashion, and with little to suggest they were in the very heart of Morocco. Only the view outside the tall windows gave away the fact that this great house was set down in one of the most unspoilt parts of this northern tip of Africa.

The view was of the splendid patio, where the fountain played, and the orange trees scented the air, and above its roof-tops rose the solid dark line of the mountains, frowning against the paling blue of the evening sky.

Jenny saw that they were in a modern lounge, with a cocktail cabinet in a corner, and some fine water-colours on the walls, and beyond it, through an arch, she saw a table laid for dinner. The table was graced with flowers and high-piled dishes of fruit, and there was a blaze of silver and cut-glass which was both dazzling and impressive.

While she stood there looking out at the patio, and Célestine sank languidly into the lap of a broad couch, a voice sounded from the doorway behind them, and Jenny whipped round.

'I'm so sorry I was not here to welcome you when you arrived,' Si Mohammed said, smiling in his most charming fashion. He wore a faultlessly cut white dinner-jacket, and his golden head shone in the last light of the setting sun. 'But I hope you found everything you wanted when you did arrive?'

Célestine, who had been yawning openly before his appearance, hastily concealed the yawn and sat up and smiled back at him brilliantly. He moved across to her and bowed over her hand, carrying it up to his lips and saluting it gallantly in the French fashion, and then he looked sideways at Jenny, who was quite unable to conceal what she felt. In fact her eyes were so large, and so accusing, that the smile he directed towards her had a touch of almost disarming gentleness in it.

'I can't tell you how delighted I am to see you here, Miss Armitage,' he told her, crossing over to the window beside which she stood and offering her his hand. 'In fact delighted does not quite describe my sensations at this moment!'

As she put her fingers into his, very reluctantly, he refrained from making the mistake of retaining them too long, and it was noticeable that he did not attempt to carry them up to his lips. But his eyes expressed something that might have been the frankest admiration while he gazed at her.

Lights were brought, for although full of so many modern innovations the *kasbah* – and Jenny was soon to learn that what she thought of as a kind of castle was in reality its Moorish equivalent – did not possess electric light, and a soft-footed servant handed round drinks before dinner was served. The dinner itself was very similar to many she had enjoyed in the St. Alais house in Marrakesh, but on this occasion she had very little appetite for it, for she had the feeling that when they set out that morning Célestine had deliberately withheld from her the name of her present host, and their destination, because she feared that the prim English governess might raise objections, and her own plans be interfered with. But the one thing which puzzled Jenny was why Célestine had wasted so little time after the departure of Max Daintry from Marrakesh before accepting, apparently, a long-standing invitation.

Or was it such a long-standing invitation?

Si Mohammed was not unaware of Jenny's bewilderment, and although he watched carefully while the meal was in progress to see that she had everything she wanted, most of his dinner-table conversation was addressed to Célestine, who, as always when she was not dining in her own house, with her own husband seated oposite to her at the table, was bright and gay, and as a consequences spectacularly lovely.

But Jenny was wondering about the children upstairs, and how they were faring, and whether supper had been taken to them, and whether perhaps they were feeling alarmed by their strange surroundings. She was also wondering about Raoul de St. Alais, and whether he knew where they were at that particular moment, and she was troubled because Célestine was so strange and secretive, and because although her host was behaving faultlessly there had been a recent occasion when he had not behaved so faultlessly – at any rate, not to her – and she could not forget the occasion.

A further surprise was in store for her when dinner was ended, and instead of being served with coffee they were requested to accompany Si Mohammed to another part of the *kasbah,* and there they were pre-sented – there was no other word for the formality of the proceeding – to an elderly, dignified man wearing the dress of his country and surrounded by true Mor-occan state. Swinging oil lamps illuminated a huge room with velvet couches ranged around it, and little low tables encrusted with mother-of-pearl and loaded with sweetmeats were drawn close to the reclining figure in the white *djellabah.*

The cowl of the *djellabah* was drawn up over a pair of fierce, proud eyes that stared hard, and in a some-what embarrassing way, at Jenny, and it was not until the introductions were over, and she realized that this was Si Mohammed's father, that she wondered why he appeared to have so little interest in Célestine, and why his glance merely flickered over her in a curiously dis-missing fashion.

Silk pouffes were brought forward for them to sit upon, and then a servant appeared with a large silver tray bearing all the appurtenances for making mint tea. The tea was served in very fine cups, and sweet-meats were offered. Célestine produced a platinum cigarette-case from her handbag and handed it round, but to Jenny's surprise neither the old Caid nor his son accepted, and as she declined herself only the Comtesse filled the slightly chill air of the great room with the aroma of choice Virginian tobacco.

Jenny sat rather awkwardly on her huge pouffe, and she noticed that the Caid flickered another glance at Célestine as she put away her lighter, and wondered whether he disapproved of women smoking so near to him, and with such an air of self-contained ease. Si

Mohammed, on the other hand, struck her as adopting a very graceful attitude, which his European dress did nothing to detract from. In the presence of his father his demeanour was one of deference and extreme respect.

The conversation – a little stilted – was carried on in French, and Jenny was asked several rather pointed questions by the Caid. He wanted to know how long she had been in Morocco, and how long she proposed to remain. His eyes had none of the brilliance of his son's, and his complexion was pale as ivory, but his almost overpowering dignity made Jenny stumble in her answers, although she sensed that his attitude was kindly.

She could feel, after the first quarter of an hour or so, Célestine's boredom rising, and when her cigarette was finished she did not hesitate to light another. They all drank the requisite three cups of mint tea essential as a sign of good manners and respect for a host, and then Si Mohammed brought the interview to an end by rising with elegant ease and suggesting that they might like to return to his own quarters.

When they stepped outside into the patio that night was dark like velvet, and the stars hung in it like lamps, but the air was decidedly chill. The Comtesse said to Jenny:

'I'll go and have a look at the children, but you two might like some fresh air. I'll send you down a wrap, Jenny.'

And before Jenny could raise any objection she had vanished under the shadowy canopy of the darkness, and Si Mohammed's voice at her elbow said softly but reassuringly:

'There is no need for you to be alarmed, Miss Jenny. I shall not repeat the mistake I made before, and while you are a guest here in my father's house you are safe from anything you might regard as unpleasant.'

Jenny could think of nothing to say in answer to such a reassurance, but she did feel a sudden sensation like relief, and there was something in his voice that convinced her he was sincere in his guarantee of good behaviour.

She permitted him to lead her forward along the paths, and when a servant appeared with her wrap she allowed him to put it about her shoulders. Above them the stars, she thought, were incredible, the scent of the starry white jasmine flowers was both heady and intoxicating, and occasionally a dove roused itself and uttered a low, soft, burbling cry from its perch under one of the colonnades.

'I hope you will remain for several days – perhaps longer,' Si Mohammed said, as they moved side by side along the paths. 'I told you about my father's house, didn't I? And I wanted you to see it. And the air is good up here.'

'You are very – remote,' Jenny found herself saying, because somehow the feeling of remoteness oppressed her.

She realized that he smiled in the darkness, and she could see the faint shine of his white teeth.

'To you, perhaps, we may seem remote, but it is not really so. A fast car and the miles to Marrakesh are eaten up in no time at all.' There was silence for a moment and then he asked: 'Do you ride?'

Jenny had to admit that she had ridden almost since babyhood, but not for the last year or so.

'Then that is good,' he answered her enthusiastically. 'I will see to it that you are provided with a mount, and in that way you will get some exercise.'

'But what about clothes?' Jenny asked. 'I haven't brought anything suitable with me.'

'We will devise something,' he said, 'or perhaps the Comtesse can solve the problem for us. She is an excellent horsewoman.'

This surprised Jenny, but she said nothing, and when he suddenly felt her shiver beside him he said with concern that she must go in.

'Our nights are very chill,' he said, 'and you must not catch a cold.'

He raised no protest when she said she would like to go straight up to her room, and the last thought which flickered through Jenny's brain before she finally fell asleep in her great bed with the enormous feather pillows and silk sheets, was that she might perhaps have been hasty in her judgment of Si Mohammed. He was, after all, of alien race, and he might have imagined her willing to be flirted with, if nothing more positive. And he seemed to have realized his mistake.

The next day, which was a wonderful day of blue skies and sunshine, and flower scents floating on the warm air, she had the two children with her about eleven o'clock in the morning when he rode into the outer courtyard where they were carelessly sauntering.

He was on a black horse, and he wore a fine white wool *djellabah* with his riding-breeches and polished boots, and a white, gold-embroidered turban. For a few moments Jenny's admiration for the sheer spectacular appeal of his appearance must have shown in her eyes, for he smiled down at her in a way that made the most of his perfect teeth, and softened the lustre of his long-lashed dark eyes. He told her:

'I have spoken to the Comtesse about riding clothes for you, and it seems that she has brought jodhpurs with her which she is very willing to lend to you. Tomorrow morning, therefore, if it is agreeable to you, I will have you called at an early hour, before the sun is hot, and we will ride together. I have a little mare which will carry you beautifully,' running his eye for a moment over her slender proportions.

Jenny thanked him, not altogether certain that she really wished to ride with him, although she thoroughly enjoyed the exercise, and she was surprised that the Comtesse had brought a pair of jodhpurs with her. Unless, of course, she had hoped to be invited to ride herself – in which case why was she sacrificing her opportunity in order that Jenny could wear the jodhpurs?

She was called the next morning (by a Moorish girl who had been deputed to wait on her and the children) at an hour when the sky was still flushed with the rosy glow of sunrise, and the air was sweet and cool like wine. She looked very slender and attractive in a silk shirt and Célestine's beautifully tailored jodhpurs, and because there was as yet little real power in the sun she contented herself with appearing in the courtyard hatless.

Si Mohammed glanced at her, and then away again

quickly, and during the ride he was unfailingly polite and attentive, but nothing more. Jenny thoroughly enjoyed the ride because for once she was doing a thing that was familiar to her, and she knew that her companion could detect nothing wrong with her horsemanship. The beauty of the Atlas at that hour of the morning was something to be remembered, and she decided that in some ways she preferred this isolated *kasbah* to the crowded lanes of Marrakesh.

She healthily enjoyed the Continental breakfast that was awaiting her when she returned, and the following morning she rode again with Si Mohammed, and Célestine assured her she could keep the jodhpurs for the remainder of their stay.

The days slipped by, and somewhat to Jenny's surprise they were very pleasant. Si Mohammed proved himself an excellent host. He kept his word, and Jenny found nothing to complain of in his manner towards her. Sometimes she thought Célestine watched them when they were together with a curious bright, speculative look in her eyes, but she had no qualms of uneasiness, and was not really sorry when the Comtesse told her she had decided there was no need for them to hurry back to Marrakesh while the Comte was away.

Jenny imagined that she received letters from him, and that he knew where they were. Neither of them discussed Max Daintry, although Célestine volunteered the information that Raoul had intended to visit their château in the south of France, and that he might linger there for a while. Its charms made it difficult for him to leave it once he was there, she told

Jenny a little dryly.

At the end of a week Jenny and the two children were returning from an excursion amongst local scenery in one of Si Mohammed's high-powered cars when she was surprised to see another car standing in the courtyard as they drove into it. It was a familiar dark crimson car with an English number plate, and in it she had once been driven to the Mamounia in Marrakesh to drink coffee with its owner. She knew she would recognize it anywhere.

Si Mohammed's eyebrows rose as he decanted his passengers alongside the dark red car, but he offered no comment. Jenny took the children up to their room and washed and tidied them, and then handed them over to the care of the Moorish girl while she went in search of their mother. Her heart was knocking uncomfortably because she knew that when she did come upon her she would not be alone, and in spite of a stern, silent lecture to herself while she washed the children, and a determination not to reveal surprise or any other emotion, her knees felt weak when she entered the patio where Célestine often walked or lounged beside the fountain.

But the patio was empty when she entered it, and the fountain was filling the air with a meaningless, musical, plashing noise. Her hand clutched at a spray of jasmine, and she stood crushing the starry white flower between her fingers without realizing what she was doing while she summoned up all her courage and looked beneath the arch into the room which had been set apart for them as a lounge, and which was part of Si Mohammed's own quarters.

The sunlight was falling so strongly in the patio that the room appeared dim, but she saw vague figures lounging on a Chesterfield couch. Voices reached her.

'I knew you'd come,' said Célestine, with a triumphant note in her voice, 'I felt absolutely certain of it! As soon as you returned and found out where we were I knew it would be only a matter of hours before you would be on your way here!'

'That was clever of you,' a mocking voice answered, 'but of course you were right. The only thing you're wrong about is that I didn't allow hours to elapse – I came at once!'

'Darling,' Célestine laughed caressingly, 'you *must* have been impatient! . . .'

Jenny turned away, still crushing the jasmine flowers. She wondered whether she had a right to intrude – or whether perhaps it would be more tactful to disappear again. And then a wave of sympathy for the Comte welled over her, and was followed by succeeding waves of self-disgust, self-pity amounting to something like anguish, and a kind of burning dislike of the Comtesse.

She felt that the Comtesse was behaving cruelly to her husband . . .

And then she heard quick footsteps on the tiled floor of the patio, and Si Mohammed Menebhi came striding towards her along one of the paths. He looked at her as if in astonishment, and then with a smile he took her arm and guided her towards the arch beyond which her employer sat with Max Daintry.

'I believe we have a visitor,' the young Moor said. 'Let's go together and meet him, shall we?'

And because she was not looking up into his face she did not see the glint in his eye, and the mild derisiveness in his voice passed her by. He was still lightly retaining her arm when they entered the room where the two who were about to be disturbed were studying one another's faces as if with interest.

CHAPTER FOURTEEN

MAX DAINTRY stood up to greet them. Although he had completed a journey by air not many hours before, and had afterwards driven a considerable number of miles through the heat of the day over uncared-for mountain roads, and had not yet had time to remove the ravages of travel, he was looking remarkably cool and self-contained and as well dressed as usual.

Jenny felt his eyes travel to her face and rest upon it with an odd, unreadable look in their grey depths, and then they passed on to the man who stood beside her. His voice was perfectly affable as he greeted them both.

'Why, hello!' he said. 'Enjoying yourself, Jenny, in these unusual surroundings? And is Si Mohammed trying to impress you with his feudalism?'

Célestine cut in and answered for her:

'Si Mohammed is not in the last feudal, and we've been having a wonderful time here, where there is every comfort save electric light.'

'Perhaps next time you come, then, Jenny, even electric light will be installed,' Max observed dryly.

Si Mohammed said in a voice that gave away absolutely nothing of what he was thinking and feeling:

'I saw your car in the courtyard, Daintry, and I gathered that our numbers were to be increased.' His eyes rested reflectively on Célestine's face. 'Shall we insist that he remains with us, Madame? For a few days, at least?'

'I have every intention of remaining – at least for tonight, if you can put me up?' Daintry returned, with cool composure. 'I know you've got enough bedrooms to accommodate a regiment, so that shouldn't seriously inconvenience you.'

'It won't,' Si Mohammed assured him politely. 'And it will, of course, be a pleasure,' he added, in smooth and polished tones.

'Then that's settled!' Célestine exclaimed, with a kind of kittenish contentment, curling up with her feet under her in a corner of the Chesterfield. 'And you can spend the evening telling us about Paris, and how gay it looked, and what exactly you did there, and why you flew back so soon. Not,' with a charming, provocative smile up at him, 'that your return isn't an extremely pleasant surprise!'

He looked down at her for a moment, and since, in her lime-green linen that made her skin look like apple-blossom by contrast, with every shining hair on her head beautifully arranged, and her greenish-golden eyes pools of mystery and seductiveness, she was the very embodiment of feminine allure, there could be no mistake about the admiration that appeared in his eyes as he studied her. Or so Jenny told herself when she noted how blank those eyes became when they returned to her own face – as if, she thought, there was nothing about her that was of any real interest to him, or which justified the faintest glimmering of approval. And she was not surprised that after that he seemed deliberately to ignore her. And although drinks were served, and they all sat about in relaxed attitudes in the cool and pleasant room, and Célestine talked a great deal, while Si Mohammed, as the host, interpolated an occasional polite remark – although even he seemed subdued, Jenny thought, and there was no pleasure in his eyes when they rested on his newest guest – the somewhat noticeable process of ignoring her continued right up until the moment when they all dispersed to change for dinner, and then he half mockingly inquired of her whether or not she could find her way to her room in such a rabbit warren, and she replied distantly that she could find her way with ease by this time.

'Which only goes to show how well you're settling down, doesn't it?' he remarked, with one corner of his mouth lifting in a faintly unpleasant smile. But she had no opportunity to answer him because Célestine urged her to hurry if she was to get the children to bed and enjoy a bath herself before dinner.

At dinner she felt very much as she had felt on her first evening in the *kasbah* – unwilling to talk because her state of mind made it impossible for her to think coherently, and unwilling to listen to the conversation of the other three because it was the kind she could not have taken part in with ease. It was sparkling conversation led by Célestine, who looked at her best in silvery silk and pearls, and touched without any real nostalgia on the Paris she insisted she adored, and where, she was just as insistent, Max Daintry, in spite of the brief duration of his visit, must have found a good deal of reward for the inconveniences of his journey.

Her tone was so arch – although her eyes watched

him carefully, even avidly – that Jenny felt a trifle sick, particularly when she saw the little half-smile Daintry gave her in return. By contrast with Si Mohammed, whose looks appeared almost feminine, he was so essentially masculine – so dominatingly masculine, that the sickness was overlaid by a kind of despairing ache. She felt she was up against something ruthless and relentless that had caught at her life merely for the calculated fun of catching at it, and that the fun would increase when she began to betray symptoms of being vanquished by the attraction she could not ignore.

She wished, as they waded through the endless meal, with its long-drawn-out courses, that she had acted upon the impulse which assailed her while she was dressing and made an excuse to stay upstairs with the children.

But Célestine, she somehow felt certain, would not have approved of that.

After dinner they paid a visit to the elderly Caid and drank the usual three cups of mint tea with him, while the last of the light died out of the sky and the African night closed down over the *kasbah*. Max Daintry obviously was well known to the Caid, and for once the old man's expression became animated while Max talked to him with fluent ease in his own tongue, and the others were so much left out of it that Célestine quickly showed her boredom and made an excuse to escape. Jenny escaped with her, and Si Mohammed was called away to some other part of the *kasbah*, so that the two women found themselves alone in the wide patio under its roof of starry sky.

'I'm going to smoke a last cigarette on my balcony,' the Comtesse said, 'and then I'm going to bed. Your admirer has probably been called away to settle a dispute in the harem, so if I were you I'd go to bed, also.'

Jenny looked shocked.

'In the – harem?' she echoed.

Célestine sent her an amused glance.

'My dear, I was only joking. Si Mohammed is as western as you or I, and as far I know he's not married. In fact, the one thing I really *do* know about him is that he is *contemplating* marriage! If there's a harem here it will contain the female belongings of his father.'

But when they had parted, and Jenny had found her way up to her room, she wished for the first time overpoweringly that they had never come to this remote *kasbah*, for the way of life led in it was not the way of life understood by herself or any member of her own race. Célestine's observation that Si Mohammed was as western as herself was probably true as far as superficial manners went, but underneath all the luxury here and the evidences of an addiction to modern ways of life there was something that was inescapably eastern.

She hoped that they would leave soon, and once they got back to Marrakesh she did not think she would remain much longer in the employment of the Comtesse de St. Alais.

Just before she started to undress she discovered in her handbag a small diamanté clip belonging to the Comtesse which she had rescued from one of the mosaic paths in the patio that afternoon, and meant to return to her employer at dinner. Thinking that Célestine might miss it she decided to slip next door and return it to her, but when she knocked on the door there was no 'Come in' in response to her knock, and when she opened the door and looked inside the room was dark and empty. The windows stood wide to the balcony, but that, too, was empty. Célestine was not smoking her final cigarette on her balcony after all!

Jenny returned to her room. From that angle of the house she could see across the patio into the rooms on the opposite side, and the huge room where they had been received by the Caid was without any sign of light. Which meant that Si Mohammed's father had retired for the night, and that Max Daintry was no longer talking to him.

And even as this realization struck her she caught the glow of cigarette ends down below her in the patio, and the murmur of voices reached her – even a faint, soft, satisfied, feminine laugh, which was undoubtedly Célestine's.

CHAPTER FIFTEEN

THE next morning Jenny found that she had little time to devote to anyone save the children, for Louis was at his most fractious, and wanting to return to his own home where all his personal things were. Simone, too, was cross and unlike herself, and Jenny decided that they had probably had rather too much sun the day before, and that it would be best to keep them in the cool of their room where she spent almost the whole of the morning reading to them and entertaining them.

At lunch she met Max Daintry for the first time that day, but apart from the merest civilities he did not take much notice of her. Nothing was said about his return to Marrakesh, so she gathered that he was remaining at the *kasbah* for another night at least. Célestine looked like a cat that had stolen the cream, and Si Mohammed was not present at the meal because whatever had demanded his presence the night before was still making demands on him, and so far no one had seen him that day.

In the afternoon Jenny rested the children for an hour, and then took them out into the patio where the colonnades cast a sufficiency of shadow, and the noise of the fountain splashing into its marble basin was a coolness in itself. Célestine and Max did not appear, but just before dinner they returned from a drive in Max's dark red car, and the Comtesse still looked as if nothing could shake her equanimity.

Jenny excused herself from having drinks with them, and lingered over the task of putting the children to bed, so that by the time she herself was ready to descend to the ground floor of the *kasbah* it was almost exactly time for the evening meal to be served. Si Mohammed, to her relief – for she had been dreading the thought of sharing what would otherwise have been a tête-à-tête meal with the other two – had returned by this time, and although he seemed rather quieter than usual, as if something was occupying his mind, at least the conversation flowed more evenly than it would otherwise have done.

They did not visit the Caid that evening for tea, but had coffee in the lounge, and again Si Mohammed politely asked if they would excuse him for a short time. Jenny hurried to make her own excuses and leave the Comtesse and Max alone together, and went up to her room to sit for a while on her balcony and watched the night close down.

But for once, after a swelteringly hot day, the night was warm, and the loneliness of her balcony, and the darkness of the room behind her, where the children slept, began to prey upon her nerves. She was feeling the need of exercise, too, since she had not even had her ride that morning and so much of the day had been devoted to sitting about in the shade and trying to keep cool that she felt she must somehow or other escape and stretch her legs.

She was afraid to descend to the main patio in case she bumped into the Comtesse and the man who was keeping her most attentive company in the absence of her husband, but there was a much smaller patio which she had discovered with the children on to which backed some rooms which were actually disused harem quarters, and she decided that there at least she was unlikely to be disturbed.

She draped a thin stole about her shoulders over her white dress, which was the one she had worn to the Benoîts' dinner-party, and stole like a shadow through the corridors which led to the disused patio. She was quite sure she was unobserved, and was pacing up and down in the deliciously cool air, and inhaling all the perfume of flowers hidden in the dusk, when in front of her there suddenly appeared a tall and interested shadow into which she all but stumbled.

'Either I come up behind you, or you charge into me!' Max Daintry remarked, and steadied her, because she had been thrown partly off her balance.

Jenny was so taken aback by this sudden appearance, and so vexed because it was the one thing she had wished to avoid, that she bit her lip hard and said nothing.

'I hope I'm not interfering with something?' he suggested blandly. 'I saw you stealing through here, and it occurred to me that you might be on your way to meet our Si Mohammed, but as he's closeted with his father at the moment that still leaves us time for a little talk. I promise you, if he appears, I'll vanish with the utmost discretion.'

Jenny could see how his eyes and his mouth mocked her through the purple gloom of the night, and all at once she was so enraged that she could only stutter a few words which made his dark eyebrows lift.

'How – how dare you? Oh, how *dare* you!' she exclaimed, turning white with anger.

'I beg your pardon?' His voice was very smooth. 'Have I said something I shouldn't have said?'

'You suggested I came here to meet Si Mohammed when you haven't the remotest right to suggest anything of the kind! When you know that I am only here at all because it was the Comtesse's wish! You, who have so far forgotten that you owe a certain amount of loyalty to a business partner, if not actually a friend, that you fly here to join his wife as soon as you get back from Paris and find that she has left Marrakesh!'

Her blood was flowing so fast, and her indignation was so high, that it was as much as she could do to get the words out clearly, and yet after the misery of the day and the night before it when she had lain wakeful until dawn – solely on his account – it was such a relief to give vent to all the poisoned doubts in her own mind that she was not intimidated by the gradual change of expression that was taking place in his face. She barely even noticed it.

But in the white starlight that was piercing the perfume-laden dusk his face was beginning to look entirely different. The mockery had vanished from his eyes, and his mouth was stern – not merely stern, but compressed into lines of utter coldness and hardness. His square jaw might have been made of steel, and when, after a moment of utter silence, he spoke, there was the ring of ice in his voice.

'Indeed?' he said, and in spite of the ice his voice was silkily soft. 'So that's what you think, is it? For such a nicely brought up young woman you have a mind like the Sunday newspapers I remember when I was in

England! They were vastly entertaining sometimes, but the entertainment was chiefly sordid. I would hardly have connected you with a desire to delve deeply into unpleasant human relationships, but you seem to have a mind that dwells on that sort of thing. Which is a pity, because you're a very attractive young woman.'

Jenny felt her breath catch in her throat, but she managed to lash out at him:

'You seem to forget that you've never made any pretence with me! From the moment we met it was easy to guess how you felt about – about the Comtesse!'

'And ever since then you've been lavishing all your pity on the Comte?'

'I think he deserves it. I think he's had to put up with a great deal.'

'From me?'

'From – as the result of an unhappy marriage!'

'Dear me!' he exclaimed. 'What a discerning child it is! You must have come up against this sort of thing before!'

'I'm thankful to say I've *never* come up against this sort of thing before!'

'And we'll hope for your sake you won't come up against it again!' Then all at once his expression grew bleak and sinister. 'But whether you're right or wrong about the reason why I came straight here from Marrakesh, there's one thing you ought to realize – that to a man of my type an attractive woman is *always* an attractive woman, and when she's young and particularly desirable I find it next door to impossible to resist the temptation to make love to her. And although – according to my own lights – I've held out rather praiseworthily in your case, because even for me you seemed just a bit *too* young for sudden assaults, now that I realize you expect nothing better of me I don't see any reason why I should deny myself any longer! If only for the excellent reason that you look not unlike Célestine—!'

And before the warning telegraph inside Jenny's brain could prepare her to meet and do battle with his intention he had swooped and caught her up violently into his arms, and she could feel herself being crushed so hard against him that for a few moments all the breath seemed driven out of her body. And then while his arms bruised her brutally his dark head was bent down, and for the first time in her life a man's hard lips took possession of hers, and the little breath that was left to her fled while all the bright stars in the sky above her wheeled and dipped crazily and she went utterly limp.

Max Daintry's own breathing was none too even when at last he lifted his head, and his grey eyes looked black in a lean face that had lost some of its tan. Jenny never afterwards knew why she didn't struggle or, given the opportunity, strike at him with her free hand, or at least make some endeavour to impress the violence of her displeasure upon him – her shocked, bemused displeasure. Unless it was because she was too bemused, and because she seemed incapable of any action just then.

And the opportunity was soon lost, for he took her back tightly into his arms and kissed her again. This time the kiss was more leisurely, and it did not deprive her of her breath, but it set every pulse in her body beating like miniature sledge-hammers, the blood sang in her ears, and she had to fight against a wild, mad impulse to cling to him and to go on clinging. Her mouth must have made some response to his, because when he looked up this time he was smiling strangely.

'Well,' he said, releasing her, 'let that be a lesson to you!'

They stared at one another in the starlight. Jenny's whole body was trembling, and even to her he looked pale – unless it *was* the starlight. But his mouth was twisted in that derisive smile she loathed.

'I—' she began. She took a deep breath and began again. 'I – I—'

And then because it was the only thing she could do she fled away from him and left him standing alone where only a moment before he had had her close in his arms.

As she fled along the path shame and bitter indignation caused her to forget all about her degrading desire to cling to him and return with rapturous abandon those shattering kisses he had pressed upon her lips, and although the lips themselves were tingling she was almost sobbing as she raced for the house and the sanctuary of her own room.

She reached the main patio and crossed it, and was turning into the maze of corridors which would eventually lead her to a staircase which wound upwards when, to her horror, she saw a figure approaching her.

But it was too late to turn b

Si Mohammed, walking
therish stride, and with his
looked up quickly when he he
He stopped, and she checked h
him.

'Is anything wrong?'

He could see at once, dim though
she was profoundly upset, and her ey
wild as they gazed at him.

She shook her head.

'No. N-nothing.'

But her voice was quivering, and he cou
breath coming quickly, and beneath the thi
of her white dress her slender breasts were r
falling in noticeable agitation.

'Nevertheless, I think something is wrong,' he
and his voice was very soft and gentle. He took
almost possessively by the arm and led her back
the broad patio, and there in the brighter light
looked at her closely. 'Tell me about it,' he invited. 'C
would you rather go inside and let me get you som
thing to drink?'

'No – no, thank you,' she answered. She was lister
ing for the footsteps that would mean that Ma
Daintry was himself crossing the patio, but there wa
no sound of them as yet. 'And if you don't mind,' wit
an appealing look up at the young Moor, 'I would lik
to go up to my room.'

'It is by no means late yet,' he returned, 'and I wa
hoping to see you before you went to bed. I have apolo
gies to make to you for absenting myself all day an

ning, but news of
last night, and
h meant that
until just
real op-

if

art-
u know
e, perhaps,
but,' he smiled
things of this sort,
ething yourself. Will
t has upset you so much
y from it?'

used her. All at once she heard
ears had been straining for, but in-
g along the path on which she and Si
u were standing, and which would mean
three would inevitably have met, they went on
an angle of the house, and Jenny breathed an
audible sigh of relief.

hammed lifted his head and listened to the
lso, and when they had died away she saw
l glitter had entered his eyes, and his voice
when he asked:

our newly arrived guest who annoyed you in
? Has Daintry done something you dis-

Jenny shook her head hastily. Max's behaviour was not a thing to be discussed with Si Mohammed.

'No, of course not!'

The Moor's eyes were on her face, and t̲ ̲ ̲ ̲ ̲ pression in them was almost painfully searching.

'It has struck me that you two are not very friendly towards one another. He is a strange man – strange and hard, and brutal if the impulse takes him. Are you quite sure he did nothing to annoy you?'

Jenny turned towards the house.

'I would like to go in – please . . .' she begged.

He put out a hand and caught hold of one of her slender wrists, and the touch of her seemed to inflame him.

'Not yet,' he said, a trifle indistinctly, 'not until I have told you something!' The close grip of his fingers tightened. 'I promised that I would not force my attentions on you while you are here, but when I find you like this – running away from a man who poses as one of your own countrymen, and who has plainly done something to either frighten or upset you – then I do not think there is any real reason why I should keep that promise! And, at least, I have no intention of frightening you – I only want to guard and protect you, and to love you all the rest of my life! I adore you . . .' His voice shook, and his eyes were glowing and lustrous as they looked down at her. She realized that although it was the last thing she wanted to do she had kindled a blazing passion in him, and all at once it had leapt up and was making the hand on her wrist shake in a storm of wild and unrepressed feeling. She was secretly appalled. 'I will not allow any man to force his unwelcome attentions on you, and I will not be happy until you are mine – and mine alone! Jenny! . . . little Jenny! . . .'

She tried to free her wrist and back away from him, but he was holding her with fingers of steel.

'You are so small – so lovely, Jenny! I have thought of nothing but possessing you ever since we first met, and if only you will marry me I will give you whatever you wish – take you wherever you wish! There shall be no question of trying to keep you away from the life with which you are familiar. You shall have absolute freedom, and whatever you desire will be my desire also. Only let me love you!'

His arms were about her, and she was fighting now to keep his face away from hers – to keep his mouth from covering hers. This was too much, she thought, anger rising in her like a flood and banishing her temporary sensation of panic, and if Max Daintry's attack upon her had been cool and deliberate and yet had left her without any desire to resist at all, this scorching ardour – and the thought passed through her brain that if one loved a man like this the flame of his passion would consume one! – had only the entirely opposite effect of making her determined to free herself in the briefest possible space of time.

'Let me go!' she cried sharply, a whole world of revulsion and anger in her clear voice as it rang out across the patio. 'Let me *go*! . . .'

'Not until I have kissed you! Not until you have agreed to marry me!'

'I have no intention of marrying you!'

'Then I will see to it that no other man has the

chance to do so!'

'You are abusing your position as host!'

'Quite right,' a deadly quiet voice said behind them, and Jenny found herself released so suddenly that she staggered back against one of the supports of the balcony above her, and Si Mohammed's eyes looked with unconcealed loathing at the man who was just a shadowy dark form in the gloom, but whose very immobility had something almost menacing about it. 'You are most decidedly abusing your position as host, and it will be as well if you don't repeat the experiment!'

Si Mohammed said thickly:

'This is the second time you have interfered. I do not forget the first time.'

'No?' Daintry murmured. 'Then let us hope there will not be a third!'

'You should confine your attentions to Madame la Comtesse de St. Alais!'

'And you,' Daintry recommended, without any expression of any kind in his voice, 'should apologize to Miss Armitage and say good night to her.

Si Mohammed looked round in a sullen way at Jenny.

'Good night, Miss Jenny,' he said, his voice as sullen as his looks. 'But since I have already asked you to marry me there is no need to apologize.'

Jenny said nothing, and Daintry stood obviously waiting for him to depart. For a few moments he hesitated, and then he turned and strode away along the path, and Daintry produced his cigarette case from his pocket and calmly lighted a cigarette.

Jenny felt she had more than enough for one night.

'The trouble with you,' Daintry remarked, as he pressed his thumb down on his lighter and caused a tiny spurt of flame to flare up between them, 'is that despite your vicarage background you're a highly inflammable young woman, and I'm not at all sure that you oughtn't to have someone to look after you — not you look after children!'

For the second time that night Jenny, after dismissing a hot retort that rose to her lips, turned and fled away from him into the dense purple gloom of the night as if she could not endure his proximity for a moment longer. And upstairs in her room, when she finally reached it, she flung herself down on her bed and shed tears of scalding humiliation that were backed by a feeling of utter despair.

But because she was afraid of disturbing the children she wept silently and dried the tears as speedily as she could, and a determination took shape in her mind to tell the Comtesse the next morning that whatever her plans were she herself would have to return to Marrakesh, and once she reached Marrakesh she would waste no time before catching the first plane home to England.

CHAPTER SIXTEEN

But in the morning, while she was struggling with the fastenings of Simone's smock, the Comtesse herself came into the room, wearing a gorgeous but flimsy wrapper, and announced that they were returning to Marrakesh directly after breakfast, and that once again Jenny could pack.

The children let out shrill squeals of delight, but their mother offered no explanation to Jenny of the reason why this apparently sudden decision had been taken. She merely looked at Jenny rather hard, and the latter wondered whether the signs of her emotional outburst of the night before were evident on her face, or whether perhaps as a result of it she looked pale and unlike herself.

But Célestine said nothing, and returned to her own room, and Jenny started thankfully to refill the suitcases they had brought with them. She could wait now until they got back to Marrakesh to tell the Comtesse that she was leaving her employment, but nothing could shake her decision now she had finally arrived at it. And having arrived at it the depths of her misery were shot through with a few faint gleams of light.

Their car was waiting for them in the outer courtyard when they reached it, but there was no sigh of the host to say good-bye. Max Daintry's rich maroon-coloured car was standing there, too, and his luggage was being stowed away in it.

Jenny and the children were to travel in the grey car. The Comtesse had arranged to travel in the red. Just before they started Max appeared, walking leisurely across the courtyard, impeccable as usual in beautifully-tailored white drill, and before he joined the Comtesse he went up to the side of the grey car and smiled and said a few words to both the children, who were bouncing excitedly up and down in it. Then he looked at Jenny with a curious expression in his dark grey eyes. But for the fact that she knew she was making a mistake she could have sworn that it was intended to be a gentle expression. It even, in some much more peculiar way, seemed to reach out at her like the beginnings of a caress.

'I hope you won't find the journey too warm,' he said. 'If these children become a nuisance we'll have them in with us, and that will give you a breather.'

'Thank you,' Jenny returned, in an icily distant voice, 'but they are my charges and I shall look after them – at least until we get back to Marrakesh. After that, since you deem me incapable of looking after other people's children, I shall be returning to England.'

He smiled – she thought there was a faint glint of humour in the smile, and then he waved his hand carelessly to her.

'Well, I should postpone deciding what you're going to do in Marrakesh until we reach there. In the meantime, we have several hours' drive ahead of us.'

And they were very long and stiflingly hot hours which wearied Jenny far more than on the outward journey. Perhaps it was because the children were par-

ticularly troublesome, full of complaints about the heat
but incapable of remaining still for even a few minutes
together. At first they were excited at the thought of
returning home, but the monotony of the scenery
palled upon them after a time, and it was as much as
Jenny could do to prevent them from becoming openly
fretful.

They kept the red car ahead of them in sight for the
first mile or so, and then it began to draw away. But all
at once they came upon it stationary in the middle of
the track, waiting, it seemed, for them to catch up. The
Comtesse, as delectable as when she started out, in a
dress of heavy white silk, with a gold bracelet loaded
with charms dangling on her slim wrist, walked across
the intervening space to Jenny and conjured up an expression of sympathy as she saw how colourless from
heat the girl looked, and that there were beads of per-
spiration on her upper lip.

'You *do* look hot,' she said — perhaps because she
knew she looked so cool herself she felt she could afford
to extend her sympathy — 'and I think you'd better let
me have these two,' indicating the children. 'Max's car
is larger than this one, and they won't be so restless if I
keep my eye upon them. And, in any case, they can
have the entire back of the car to themselves.'

Although Jenny protested the children were whisked
away from her, and just before he climbed back into his
driving-seat Max looked across at her and smiled.
There was no doubt about it, it *was* a friendly smile,
but it won no response from Jenny. She felt that never
again would she smile at Max Daintry, and never
again did she want to exchange even a few words of

conversation with him.

This time, when they started off, she had the back seat to herself, and at least she was free from the necessity of constantly watching the children. She must have dozed for a short while, for when she opened her eyes there was no sign of the other car, but they were still high up in the mountains. In fact, they even seemed to her to be climbing, which struck her as odd, because what they really should be doing was descending. On the outward journey they had climbed steeply, but the road back to Marrakesh should be downhill almost all the way.

But there was no doubt about it, they *were* climbing. Jenny leant forward and addressed the impassive chauffeur's back, but at first he ignored her halting Arabic, and then when she addressed him in French he slightly shrugged his shoulders. But Jenny persisted in Arabic.

'Where are we going? This doesn't seem to be the right way! Where is the other car?'

The chauffeur answered at last, in a surly fashion.

'The other car is much faster than this. But soon we catch up with it.'

'I don't believe we're on the right road,' Jenny said.

Again the chauffeur shrugged.

'The lower road is blocked by a fall of stone. It was necessary to take the upper road.'

Jenny lay back against the seat, but she was puzzled by the strangeness of the light. She must have slept for much longer than she thought, for unless she was very much mistaken this was afternoon light, and the morn-

168

ing was well behind them. When she looked at her watch she discovered that it had stopped, but the heat of the car was insufferable, and that meant they had been travelling for hours.

She watched the road still winding upwards, and then all at once it dipped down steeply into a valley. Jenny could recognize none of the scenery, but the loneliness was like a living thing pressing in on them, and uneasiness began to throb in her veins. For the first time the fact that Célestine had relieved her of the children struck her as odd, for in the weeks that she had worked for the Comtesse she had never known her display so much consideration before. Unless it was Max who had insisted that she be relieved of them when she had slept scarcely a wink the night before! But somehow she could not believe that it was Max, although before they started off he had suggested that they might be too much for her.

She wished she could make the chauffeur talk, but he resisted all further attempts to extract information from him. And as the sharp descent continued it was not long before they were out on an open, dusty plain. It was not so much desert as a wilderness of sandy ground, with some thwarted-looking vegetation breaking its surface here and there, and occasional stunted groups of palms.

Jenny's heart began to fail her when she realized that, although they were travelling at terrific speed in spite of the appalling surface of the road, the light that she had known to be afternoon light began to be tinged with the red-gold of early evening. And it was evident that they were miles from Marrakesh. The type of scenery she was viewing on either hand had nothing in common with the way back to Marrakesh, and where there were groups of palms there were occasionally little clusters of mud hovels like primitive *kasbahs,* and white painted wells. The landscape was sun-parched, monotonous and austere, and the skyline receded indefinitely.

Jenny gave up speaking with exasperated sharpness to the driver, but inside herself she knew that something was very, very wrong. Forty-eight hours before she might have been considerably more alarmed than she was, but physical weariness, amounting almost to exhaustion – sickness of heart – in some way kept even acute curiosity at bay. She only knew that wherever she was being taken someone had planned it all beforehand, and since it was the Comtesse's car in which she was travelling, and her chauffeur who was at the wheel, she was still in some sort of contact with the St. Alais family.

Even when the sun went down, and the night closed in, and instead of being fiercely warm it began to grow bitterly cold, she still refused to allow herself to think of Max Daintry. One side of her brain felt almost numb about him, and the other half shrank from the thought of him. Whatever fate was in store for her she had no desire at all that he should ever learn of it.

At last the car stopped in what appeared to be the very centre of a village, although in the white starlight there were only one or two vague, muffled shapes moving in the shelter of the palms. The chauffeur left his driving seat and came round and held open her door for her, but she was almost too stiff to alight.

When at last she managed to do so her legs bent under her, and but for the chauffeur's hand under her arm she would have fallen.

She was faint with hunger, ravaged by thirst that had been tormenting her for hours, and the bitter coldness of the night and her inadequate clothing set her teeth chattering violently. When she found herself inside a mud-walled building with only a light provided by a kind of primitive wick floating in a saucer of oil, and standing on a table with a brass tray on the top of it, the one thing she noticed and felt glad of was that there was something like a divan in a corner, and all she craved to do was to sink down on it.

The chauffeur departed, and a woman entered. She wore the usual shapeless *haik* of Arab women, but she was not veiled. She was also very pretty, or so she appeared in the light of the oil lamp, and she seemed quite friendly. She brought Jenny a pitcher of water and a brass bowl in which to wash the dust and grime of the road from her hands and face if she wished, and a tray of thick, black, heavily-sweetened coffee. She also indicated that the divan was to be her bed, and that she could make use of it as soon as she wished.

Jenny never forgot that night – or, rather, she never forgot the odd, confused sensations that were all she was aware of. She had probably, as she realized afterwards, got a touch of sun, but instead of being greatly concerned at finding herself where she was, all she wanted to do was to sink into deep and dreamless slumber. She even neglected to make use of the bowl of water, but she drank the coffee thirstily. Then she crawled to the divan and lay down on it, and within a matter of minutes a blanketing unawareness of anything was upon her.

When she opened her eyes it was next day and high noon. There were sounds of lazy activity outside the hut, and looking from the window she saw women drawing water at a well while men lounged in the shade. The sun struck down fiercely across the pleasantly meandering village street, and by contrast with its white-hot light the shadows cast by the palm trees were almost inkily black. There were several children playing a game which seemed to be hopscotch right outside the window, and Jenny watched them in a dazed state of unbelief.

The woman who had brought her the water and the coffee the night before reappeared with further refreshments on a tray, and this time, to Jenny's infinite relief, instead of the sickly coffee there was mint tea. She had never formed a great partiality for mint tea, but now she drained the pot dry, and would have willingly drunk more if it had been available. But she found that she had absolutely no appetite for the highly spiced *kus-kus* – a native dish – which accompanied the mint tea, and indeed she was almost revolted by the thought of eating anything at all.

This time the Arab girl was without her *haik*, and her hair was dressed in dozens of little plaits intertwined with beads and ornaments. She had large and very beautiful eyes, and towards Jenny her manner was quite subservient. Jenny managed to make her understand that she would like more water to wash with, and when it was brought, together with a couple of small hand-embroidered towels, she started on the difficult task of trying to extract information from the girl. But here again there was either no real knowledge, or the girl had been forbidden to talk. She made expressive gestures with her shoulders and spread her hands, but that was all Jenny could get out of her, and she finally gave up the attempt to discover why she was where she was, and by whose order she had been brought there.

If it was the Comtesse – and it was the Comtesse's car that had brought her there, although both it and the chauffeur had now disappeared – then the reason for it was inexplicable. It was certainly not with the sanction of the Comte, even if he had returned from Paris. And that left Si Mohammed. But she preferred not to dwell upon the thought of Si Mohammed in connection with this extraordinary abduction to which she had been subjected, because the possibilities arising out of such a thought were altogether too unpleasant.

Instead, having restored a certain amount of her personal freshness by washing in the inadequate bowl, she was glad to discover that she still had her handbag with her, and painstakingly made up her face and restored order to her hair. She did this with great care, largely to occupy herself, and because now at last a feeling of growing panic was doing its best to take possession of her, and she knew that she had to conquer it somehow or other.

She spent the afternoon lying on the divan while the little room sweltered, and because the door to it was kept securely locked the only air that reached her was through the high, glassless barred window. She watched the golden light turn to the crimson of sunset, the deep, staring blue of the sky become dimmed, and the first stars appear, and as still no one came near to disturb her, her fears, instead of becoming lulled, began to surge up in her like hysteria.

It was bad enough to be captive, but it was dreadful not to know anything at all about the reason why she was confined to a mud-walled room in the centre of a primitive African village where, at sunset, drums began to throb, and she heard the thin crying of a reed pipe which, even in the security and comfort of her room in Marrakesh, had filled her with nameless dislike and dread whenever she heard it.

She began to think more and more of Max Daintry. He had asked her to go back to England. She wished she knew now *why* he had wanted her to go back, and whether after all she had made a mistake in attributing his anxiety to be rid of her, or so it had seemed, to purely personal reasons. She tried to recall the picture of his face, with its strong jaw and utterly firm mouth and eyes that never wavered. Surely it was not with any sanction of his that she was where she was? – even though he had kissed her as if he despised her, and she sensed that for some reason he was irritated by her.

But he *had* kissed her! . . . In the loneliness of her hut she recalled those two, quite dissimilar kisses he had given her, the feel of his arms while he held her, and for the first time she acknowledged how bitterly envious she was of Célestine, who could command his kisses as a kind of right, and who perhaps planned one day to be free of the Comte and marry Max.

When darkness fell she was brought a light, and she

was glad of it, because she no longer felt in the least sleepy, and to have lain staring into the darkness under such circumstances would have shaken her courage considerably. It was already beginning to crack a little – and she had a desperate fear that the crack might widen.

But after a time the lamp burned itself out, and she had to lie in darkness. She lay staring at the tiny square of her window, watching the stars blazing away up in the deep night sky, trying not to remember where she was, and wondering how soon it would be dawn, and then once more morning.

If she had to endure another day like the previous one she felt she would go mad.

Long after midnight – or she felt certain it must be long after midnight – she heard a car stop outside the hut. The noise of it was unmistakable, for she had heard nothing like it all day, and the quick slam of the door was just as unmistakable. Someone was approaching the hut, and was engaging someone else in conversation. Jenny could follow none of it, and the voices were too low to be recognizable. But after a long-drawn-out agony, which was probably no more than a minute at most, a key grated in the lock of her door and it was flung open. Jenny crouched on the foot of her bed and waited in the darkness for the first sight of the one who entered. She had a vague impression of a tall white form, and eyes that peered towards her in the starlight, and then a voice spoke her name, sharply.

'Jenny! . . . Jenny, are you there? Jenny! . . .'

Jenny got slowly on to uncertain feet, and she felt herself swaying slightly as she did so. It couldn't be

Max's voice! – it *couldn't*! . . . And then she answered weakly:

'I'm here! . . .'

He took two strides towards her, and she felt arms reach out and catch at her, and she was supported by the very fierceness of that hold. For the first time she heard Max Daintry's voice shaken, in fact shattered, and quite unlike itself.

'Oh, Jenny!' he exclaimed. 'Thank heaven I've found you! I—'

And then she hurled herself against his chest and burst into uncontrollable sobbing.

CHAPTER SEVENTEEN

WHEN later she managed to calm down sufficiently she found that she was seated on the side of the divan bed, that Max Daintry was seated beside her, and that she was held comfortingly close in his arms and his hand was stroking her hair. She did not realize it, but it was not a particularly steady hand.

'I'm so sorry!' she apologized, over and over again. 'I'm so terribly sorry – I ought not to behave like this! . . .'

'Darling, don't,' he said at last, and she was not quite sure whether this was a kind of delirium – if it was, she hoped it would go on for ever and ever. 'Jenny, my precious girl, I know you've had a ghastly time, but I'll soon have you out of this, and then you'll forget all about it. But don't keep saying you're sorry for shedding a few tears – I only wish I could have got here before and spared you some of them!'

Jenny put back her head and looked up at him uncertainly.

'It – it is you, isn't it?' she asked. 'I'm not dreaming. . . ?'

'No, darling, you're not dreaming. It's me all right.'

She could see his eyes smiling down at her in the starlight, and it was a smile such as she had sometimes imagined she might one day see in them. It was a smile and a look that made her catch her breath.

'How did you know where I was?' she asked.

'We won't go into that now,' he returned. 'I've got to get you away from here as quickly as possible, and we mustn't waste any time. But you'll hear all about it at the first opportunity.' He dried her wet face with his crisp pocket-handkerchief. 'Shall I tell you something?' he asked hoarsely. 'Something that can't wait?'

'Yes,' she breathed, feeling as if her heart turned over.

'The past forty-eight hours have been the worst I've ever lived through. And if I hadn't found you I think I'd have gone stark, staring mad!'

'W-why?' she barely whispered, and although she was quite unaware of it her fingers were clinging to him.

'Why?' He put his own fingers under her chin and lifted it, and through the gloom he gazed at her as if he could never gaze hard and long enough. 'Because I've had to live to thirty-five to fall madly, desperately, hopelessly in love with a small girl who has always thought the worst of me! ... Because even if she does think the worst of me I still can't do anything about my love, and I'll just have to beg her to try and change her mind about me!'

'Oh!' Jenny exclaimed, and there was a sharp note like anguish in her voice, because although she was quite sure now that this was delirium the undisguised hurt in his tone pierced her like a knife-thrust. 'Don't say that! Please!' she begged. 'I can't think why I – why I was so utterly stupid! – but I've loved you so much ever since I've known you, and been so hopelessly miserable that at least I've been punished!'

'Oh, Jenny my sweet, why didn't I realize it before!' For a few moments that last night in the patio of the Caïd's *kasbah* was recalled as he strained her so fiercely to him that she found it difficult to breathe. 'If only I had I might have saved you this horrible experience – and I was a brute to you only two nights ago! I wanted to hurt you, and I think I did, didn't I, darling? You looked so white and bewildered, and your lips gave you away – just a little!'

He started to grope for them hungrily, and she turned them up to him eagerly. This time the kiss was so utterly perfect that they were both shaking when they drew apart, and his eyes devoured her.

'Sweetheart, we must go!' He stood up and drew her with him. 'Have you got anything in the nature of a wrap?'

'No.' She shook her head. 'I'm just as I – as I was when we started out the other day!'

'Never mind. I've some rugs in the car, and I'll see that you're not cold.'

He seemed to stand listening for a few moments, and then he moved towards the door.

'How did you get the girl to let you in?' Jenny whispered, keeping close to him.

'Oh, that was comparatively easy. But don't say anything, darling.' He opened the door, and for the first time in many hours Jenny stood upon the threshold of freedom, and the sweet, cool scents of the night came at her in an intoxicating rush. She saw the dark shape of a car standing near to them. Max swung open the nearest door and she climbed into the seat beside the driving-seat. He got in himself and handed her a rug to drape about her shoulders, and then he pressed the self-starter button and the car responded immediately. They crawled silently down the long village street, with the light of the late rising moon bathing them in a flood of brilliant silver, and the palm trees rustling on either side of them.

And then the car picked up speed, still without making any more noise than that of a cat contentedly purring, and they shot away over the broad face of the desert, with the nose of the car turned in the direction of Marrakesh.

Jenny settled down in a kind of bewildered bliss beside the white figure at the wheel, huddling the rug about her shoulders because the night air was very keen. When they had been travelling for about ten minutes, and the Arab village was well behind them, Max asked softly:

'Are you all right, Jenny?'

'Yes, thank you – perfectly all right!'

She felt his hand feeling for hers, and their fingers locked closely for about half a minute. He said in a voice so filled with tenderness that only a few days ago she would not have connected it with him.

'When we've got just a little farther on our way I'll stop and tuck you up more warmly, my darling. You mustn't be cold, and you've had such a nightmarish time. That hut was—!' She saw him bite his lip – tear at it as if anger was coursing through him in an almost ungovernable fashion, and his face looked white and set in the moonlight. 'How were you looked after? Were you fed all right?'

'Oh, yes – but I wasn't very hungry,' she admitted,

in a voice that sounded small and pathetic.

He swore, and then apologized.

'Were you very frightened?'

'I was beginning to feel frightened just before you came.'

'And when I came—'

She sent him a sideways look.

'I'd have endured the whole thing over again just for the absolute joy of having you come in the way you did!'

'*Darling*,' he said, and then they were silent while the car covered several miles.

Presently Jenny realized they were nearing the foot-hills of the Atlas, and all at once the car came to rest, and the engine died into silence. Max reached for a rug on the seat behind him and tucked it in carefully over her knees, and then he found a cushion and stuffed it behind the soft gold-bronze of her hair. He touched the hair gently with his fingers.

'I said you had red hair, didn't I?' he whispered. 'And so you have – just a touch of red. And that's why, although you look cool and sweet as a flower, you're my own beloved woman when you're in my arms!'

He resisted the temptation to draw her fiercely back into them, because her small face looked white and tired, and the large eyes were heavily underlined by shadows. He leant forward and kissed them gently, lingeringly.

'Jenny, sweetheart, have you formed any theories at all about this kidnapping of you?'

'Was it – Si Mohammed?' she asked.

'It was,' frowning at the wheel, 'but even he

wouldn't have thought up the thing entirely alone. He's young, and rather primitive, and you were a tantalizing prize, and I've no doubt he thought himself very much in love with you. But Célestine – Célestine devised the whole thing!' His fingers gripped hard at the wheel, and he stared away over the desert. 'I don't suppose it's easy for you to understand the type of woman Célestine is – possessive, hard, determined never to be frustrated if she can help it! She – I – I've known her since her teens, and I've few illusions where she is concerned. But although I'm not a saint, Jenny – perhaps very far from it! – I've never made love to her. Do you believe that?'

Jenny whispered back weakly that she did.

He looked at her yearningly.

'You've got to believe it, because it's true. And there must be no more doubts between us two. Célestine would have had it otherwise, I know – and I think she hated you so much that she jumped at the opportunity to get you out of her way. She thought if Si Mohammed married you I would never be able to have you, and so she did her utmost to throw the two of you together. And before we left the *kasbah* she had persuaded him to try force. That was why it was her car that took you all the way to that Arab village. And but for the fact that the old Caid was taken seriously ill on the morning we left, Si Mohammed would have been after you to pick up his prize before I could have reached your side!'

She could tell by the way a quiver invaded his voice, and by the faint whitening of his knuckles as his hand gripped the wheel, how such a thought upset him, and her hand reached out and slipped inside his arm. He looked down at it and crushed it against him convulsively.

'Darling, I'm taking you to Lady Berringer now — you'll be safe there until I can make other arrangements for you.' He looked at her quickly, and she wondered what those other arrangements would be, but the exhaustion in her face prevented him from telling her there and then. Instead he kissed her hand, tucked it inside the rug, and started up the car once more. 'Until we're through these mountains I won't be really happy. This is still very much Si Mohammed's country. But don't get the wrong ideas, darling — now that I know you're really mine no man will ever take you away from me! No man, under any circumstances!'

The car moved gently forward, and she asked because she simply had to know:

'How did you find out where I was?'

Max did not look round at her as he answered:

'Shall we say I forced the truth, and nothing but the truth, out of Célestine! I might even have frightened her a little! . . .'

CHAPTER EIGHTEEN

THE next evening at dusk a big red car drew up outside the Mamounia, and Max Daintry, very trim and immaculate in evening things, alighted and went into the hotel. When he emerged Jenny was with him, wearing her white sprigged evening dress, and a stole about her shoulders. She looked as if she had enjoyed a very long and refreshing sleep, and her eyes were bright.

Max handed her into the car, and then got into the driving-seat, and the car moved away. He said to her softly:

'I'm taking you to a Moorish restaurant, which I think you'll like. You've never been there before.'

'I've never been out to dinner with you before,' she answered, and even as she did so every pulse in her body leapt, for she was dining alone with him to-night.

'But you have had lunch with me in my own house.'

'Yes.' She looked sideways at him with adorable shyness. 'I liked it – your house, I mean.'

'That's just as well,' he told her, 'because unless you've changed your mind about me it will be your own house soon – *very* soon, I hope!'

She felt as if her breath was temporarily suspended in her throat. Her voice trembled as she answered:

'I couldn't change my mind about you – ever!'

'And fortunately ever's a very long time,' the man

returned quietly.

The car slid silently down the long, palm-tree-bordered Avenue du Maréchal Lyautey, and then, while the night closed down and the huge Moroccan stars appeared, wound in and out of the labyrinth of cobbled lanes and narrow streets that made up the *medina*. After a while it plunged into an even deeper wilderness of palms called the *palmeraie*, and in this jungle world of silence which was yet so close to all the activity of the French city, it slid suddenly to a halt.

Jenny looked at her companion in the dim light and reminded him that he had said they were going to a Moorish restaurant.

'We are, my beloved, when I've had an opportunity to kiss you,' he answered dryly, 'and to convince myself that our journey back to Marrakesh last night was not a dream!'

He switched off his engine and turned and looked at her. Jenny felt as if a flame rose up in her and quivered along every nerve centre of her body, and at the same time her bones turned to water. She seemed to melt into his arms when they came out to claim her, and when his lips touched hers she shut her eyes and felt waves of ecstasy break over her.

The minutes passed, and the night wind soughed softly through the palms, a dog barked, and slippered footfalls passed near to them. Starlight pierced the palm leaves and painted a silver web on the roof of the car.

Max held Jenny possessively close. With one hand he stroked her bright hair.

'Darling,' he said softly, at last. 'Jenny!'

She looked up at him with bemused eyes, and when he looked into them all the depth and extent of her love gleamed at him from under her white eyelids.

'Yes?' she whispered.

'Jenny! You'll marry me at once, won't you? There can't be any waiting. For one thing, I couldn't wait, and for another there's no reason why we should. I want you in my care – in my house, where I can keep an eye on you all the time, and where I know you'll be safe! And perhaps one day we'll go home to England and I'll show you the house I told you about, where you'll fit in so perfectly. We may even go quite soon. But, in the meantime, do you think you can put up with Marrakesh?'

'I could put up with anywhere so long as I was with you,' she answered.

He kissed her lingeringly.

'But you don't dislike Marrakesh so very much, do you – in spite of your experiences over the past few days?'

'I shall forget all about them,' Jenny told him, but she wondered what had happened when he went to the St. Alais house in the *medina* to fetch all her things and tell Célestine that she would never be returning to look after the children. Célestine must have felt that she had gambled recklessly and lost – although she had been gambling on something that would never be hers in any case. So she had really lost nothing at all!

Max read her thoughts, and he said quietly:

'Célestine even appeared surprised that I wasn't taking you back to her. She put quite a good face on it! Sent her maid to pack up your things, and asked me to let you know that if there is anything she can do for you at any time she will always be glad to do it.' He smiled strangely when he added: 'When I told her I was marrying you soon she even offered to give a party for you if you'd like one! What a woman! – and very, very French!'

'What about the Comte?' Jenny asked. 'Has he returned yet?'

'No, but he is expected back quite soon. Poor Raoul – why he married a woman like Célestine I shall never know. It was a mixture of fire and water. I honestly believe that Lady Berringer had it in mind that he might one day divorce Célestine – probably citing me! – and marry you! I'm sure she thought you'd make a much better Comtesse, and a better mother for Louis and Simone, than Célestine!'

Jenny felt her face colouring brilliantly.

'How – how can you say a thing like that?' she demanded. 'It's no use bringing a divorce action unless you're sure of unfaithfulness – and Célestine is fond of her children in her way. Apart from you I don't think anyone could ever cause her to risk losing her present security, and so far as you're concerned the Comte couldn't possibly—'

'No, darling, he couldn't,' he half laughed against her ear. 'But you wouldn't have been so certain of that – say – three weeks ago, would you?'

She looked up at him with distressed eyes.

'Will you ever forget that I was so stupid?' And then, with a spurt of spirit: 'But all the same – Célestine *is* beautiful, and you *did* kiss me believing I was her! You must have kissed her before that!'

'Must I?' His eyes were twinkling wickedly, and deliberately confusing her. 'Perhaps just once or twice – on the hair! I like red hair!'

He buried his lips in her hair.

She thrust away from him.

'Would you like it if I had allowed Si Mohammed to kiss me that night?'

She saw his face darken until it was almost frightening.

'If he had, I think – I think I would have been sorely tempted to kill him! As it is he'll keep out of my way in future.' Then his arms drew her close again, and his voice was all tender urgency. 'Jenny, sweetheart, you're the only woman I've ever loved – the only woman I've ever asked to marry me! And I'm going to marry you soon – so soon that I feel light-headed at the thought. Oh, Jenny, how much do you love me?'

'Enough to feel light-headed at the thought of marrying you, too,' Jenny answered, with a funny wavery note in her voice which proved that she really was a little light-headed.

January Paperbacks

THAT SUMMER OF SURRENDER *Rebecca Caine*
Perdita and her stepmother got on like a house on fire—it was Blake Hadwyn who caused Perdita all the trouble!

LOVE AND LUCY BROWN *Joyce Dingwell*
Lucy was looking forward to her new job—but she didn't get a very warm welcome ...

DARLING JENNY *Janet Dailey*
The last thing Jenny had wanted was to fall in love—with the man who loved her sister!

THE IMPOSSIBLE MARRIAGE *Lilian Peake*
How could Beverley and Grant possibly get married as that will stipulated? They couldn't stand each other!

AUTUMN CONCERTO *Rebecca Stratton*
Jacques Delange got Ruth a job with his uncle Hugo—who wasn't quite as charming as his nephew!

THE NOBLE SAVAGE *Violet Winspear*
Snobbish Mrs. du Mont wanted to get to know the Conde Estuardo Santigardas de Reyes. But he was more interested in her companion ...

PROUD CITADEL *Elizabeth Hoy*
Judy had burned her boats by marrying Glen. And then another woman came along to cause trouble.

WHITE HEAT *Pamela Kent*
Karin hadn't taken to Grant Willoughby. And now she was stranded with him in the middle of the Indian Ocean!

A PAVEMENT OF PEARL *Iris Danbury*
Holford Sinclair didn't want Rianna interfering in his underwater expedition. How dared he treat her like this?

HIGH-COUNTRY WIFE *Gloria Bevan*
Roseanne shouldn't have made the mistake of getting too involved with four-year-old Nicky. Look where it had landed her!

25p net each

DID YOU MISS OUR 1974 CHRISTMAS PACK?

THE JAPANESE SCREEN
Anne Mather

Susannah met and fell in love with Fernando Cuevas in London. She little thought when she travelled to Spain to work for a wealthy family that the child she had come to teach was Fernando's child and that she would be meeting Fernando himself sooner than she had expected ...

THE GIRL AT GOLDENHAWK
Violet Winspear

Jaine was accustomed always to take back place to her aunt, a spoilt darling of the London stage, and her glamorous cousin Laraine. As it seemed only natural to *them* that Jaine should take on the difficult task of explaining to Laraine's wealthy suitor that she had changed her mind about the marriage, Jaine nerved herself to meet the arrogant Pedro de Ros Zanto. Was there a surprise in store?

PRIDE AND POWER
Anne Hampson

Leona's pride suffered a tremendous blow when she discovered that the beautiful mansion and the prosperous farm that went with it belonged not as she thought to her grandmother, but to the forbidding Konon Wyndham, a man she had always hated. Now he had the power to humble her. Would he use it?

SWEET SUNDOWN
Margaret Way

Ever since she was a little girl Gabriele had been promised a trip to Sundown, the lovely old mansion where her mother had been born. And now she was going there at last at the invitation of her glamorous aunt Camilla. What would the visit bring Gabriele in the way of a new life ... and a new love?

Available at £1.00 net per pack
either from your local bookshop or if in difficulty from
Mills & Boon Reader Service,
P.O. Box 236, 14 Sanderstead Rd.,
S. Croydon, CR2 OYG, Surrey, England.

Your copy of the Mills & Boon Magazine —
'Happy Reading'

If you enjoyed reading this MILLS & BOON romance and would like a list of other MILLS & BOON romances available, together with details of all future publications and special offers, why not fill in the coupon below and you will receive, by return and post free, your own copy of the MILLS & BOON magazine —*'Happy Reading'*.

Not only does it list nearly 400 MILLS & BOON romances which are available either from your local bookshop or in case of difficulty from MILLS & BOON READER SERVICE, P.O. BOX 236, 14 Sanderstead Road, S. Croydon, CR2 OYG, Surrey, England, but it also includes articles on cookery and craft, a pen-pals scheme, letters from overseas readers, plus an exciting competition!

For those of you who can't wait to receive our catalogue we have listed over the page a selection of current titles. This list may include titles you have missed or had difficulty in obtaining from your usual stockist. Just tick the selection your require, fill in the coupon below and send the whole page to us with your remittance including postage and packing. We will despatch your order to you by return!

Please send me the free MILLS & BOON magazine ☐
Please send me the titles ticked ☐

I enclose £   (No C.O.D.) Please add 2p per book for postage and packing (10p if you live outside the U.K.)

Name ....Miss/Mrs.

Address ....

City/Town ....

County/Country ....Postal/Zip Code...............

MB 12/74

Your Mills & Boon Selection

☐ 615
THE OTHER TURNER GIRL
Ruth Clemence

☐ 635
IMMORTAL FLOWER
Elizabeth Hoy

☐ 656
THE MILL IN THE MEADOW
Jane Donnelly

☐ 665
IF LOVE BE LOVE
Flora Kidd

☐ 688
HAPPY WITH EITHER
Ruth Clemence

☐ 757
THE ONE AND ONLY
Doris E. Smith

☐ 764
AN ECHO OF SPRING
Lucy Gillen

☐ 778
FAMILIAR STRANGER
Lilian Peake

☐ 789
WHITE HUNTER
Elizabeth Hoy

☐ 798
ERRANT BRIDE
Elizabeth Ashton

☐ 801
A SONG BEGINS
Mary Burchell

☐ 807A
ROMAN SUMMER
Jane Arbor

☐ 809
WINTER OF CHANGE
Betty Neels

☐ 812
BELOVED ENEMY
Mary Wibberley

☐ 815
THE YOUNG DOCTOR
Sheila Douglas

☐ 817
WINDWARD CREST
Anne Hampson

☐ 825
THE CRESCENT MOON
Elizabeth Hunter

☐ 827
BEWILDERED·HEART
Kathryn Blair

☐ 834
MIRANDA'S MARRIAGE
Margery Hilton

☐ 839
STARS THROUGH THE
MIST
Betty Neels

☐ 841
THE NIGHT OF THE
HURRICANE
Andrea Blake

☐ 852
STORM OVER MANDARGI
Margaret Way

☐ 857
LUCIFER'S ANGEL
Violet Winspear

☐ 863
CINDERELLA IN MINK
Roberta Leigh

☐ 868
THE HONEY IS BITTER
Violet Winspear

All priced at 20p. Please tick your requirements and
see over for handy order form.